"Do I make ⁻   with a faint smile.

Feeling he.   away.

"Somewhat, yes.   uck in her throat and came   ned and thin.

"You make me   ง. The smile broadened, causing Danny to ɑ   che words.

She snorted in disbelief. "I can't believe how I feel around you," she blurted and turned away again when she realized what she had said. She felt Maureen's hip touch her own and she sucked air in sudden panic.

"How do I make you feel?" Maureen purred in Danny's ear.

"Like I'm fifteen." She looked into Maureen's eyes, now at a distance of inches. "You look like you find me amusing. Do you?"

Maureen's arm closed over Danny's shoulders. "You're very attractive."

"You're more attractive." Her heart hammered against her chest, pounded in her throat. Danny swallowed to clear the ringing in her ears.

"Do you mind if I kiss you?"

"Do I act like I mind?" She watched Maureen's face close in on her own and shut her eyes as the dark eyes converged. . . .

FRIENDS AND LOVERS

A ROMANCE BY

JACKIE CALHOUN

The Naiad Press, Inc.
1993

Printed in the United States of America on acid-free paper
First Edition

Edited by Christine Cassidy
Cover design by Pat Tong and Bonnie Liss
    (Phoenix Graphics)
Typeset by Sandi Stancil

Library of Congress Cataloging-in-Publication Data

Calhoun, Jackie.
    Friends and lovers / by Jackie Calhoun.
        p.   cm.
    ISBN 1-56280-041-8
    1. Lesbians—United States—Fiction.   I. Title.
PS3553.A3985F74   1993
813'.54—dc20   93-24912
                                                                              CIP

About the Author

Jackie Calhoun Smith makes her home in Wisconsin. The author of *Lifestyles, Second Chance,* and *Sticks and Stones,* she is now working on her sixth novel.

I

Snow swirled around Danny's booted feet and coated her cross-country skis. Standing in a white world of bitter cold at the top of a long climb, pausing to catch her breath, she smiled in pleasure at her surroundings — the mounds of snow concealing the ground, clumps of white caught in drooping evergreens, the black trunks and branches of deciduous trees reaching toward a pale blue sky. Shivering a little, she listened to the wind howling through the pines — a lonely sound, even in the summer. In winter it symbolized cold.

How could she have left, she wondered. How could she have taken so many years to find her way back to Wisconsin again? Ahead, the trail plunged steeply out of sight.

Huffing noisily, Kara joined her on the ridge. "Feels like the top of the world, doesn't it?" she gasped.

"It does," Danny agreed.

"What's it like ahead?" Kara glided forward until she stood parallel to Danny, whose skis occupied the tracks. "Why did we take the expert trails, Danielle?" she wailed.

Danny felt a smile spread across her face. "You didn't have to follow."

"You know I can't read a map." Kara, shorter and rounder than Danny, peered up at her through frosty brows.

Leaning on her poles, loath to leave the top of the ridge, Danny returned the look. There were a lot of years between them. She hated to think how many. "Why did I ever think it would be better to live somewhere else, Kara?"

Kara looked away. "You *said* you wanted to leave Edgemont and go where no one knew you."

"I was a fool." Skiing to where the run dropped off into space, she turned and smiled encouragingly. "You ready for this?"

Kara shook her head. "As ready as I'm ever going to be. It'll be one long scream."

Realizing they should have taken an intermediate trail, Danny suggested, "You can walk down, you know. There's no shame in that."

Kara lifted her chin. "If you can do it, my friend, so can I."

Danny crouched over her skis on the long run down, the cold and speed bringing tears to her eyes. She waited at the bottom as Kara careened after her, shrieking around the turns. "That was brave," she said dryly as Kara landed in a heap at her feet. "Are you okay?"

"I hate you," was Kara's comment. She struggled upright and they set off, skis squeaking in the deep tracks, poles crunching through the crust of snow.

A chickadee called loudly from a bare branch and a nuthatch muttered as it made its way headfirst down the trunk of the same tree. A chorus of crows cawed from the woods to the left, as if they had located an owl and were sounding their displeasure.

Planting a pole, Danny kicked back with one foot, driving the other forward — pole, kick, glide. The rhythm propelled her at an amazing speed along the snowy trails. Enjoying the power in her legs and arms, she vaguely realized she was lengthening the distance between herself and Kara.

As she shot forward, Danny wondered why it was she and Kara reunited as if they had never been apart, no matter the amount of time or miles that had separated them. They seemed to pick up conversations right where they had left them, the two of them chattering to fill in the blanks.

Thirty-nine years old, in the middle of a divorce, a sullen sixteen-year-old daughter in tow, Danny had returned to her hometown a few weeks ago. Tracy took form in her mind: slender and on the tall side, with long reddish-brown wildly curling hair, hazel eyes framed by long lashes, a pouting mouth, a few zits. In all fairness, no teenager willingly left her friends and traveled with one parent — the one she

3

adjudged guilty of the parental split, of disrupting her life — to a new school in a strange (to her) city. Tantrums were to be expected, sullen silences too. But the kid had her good attributes. Danny focused on these and came up with zip. Perhaps it had to do with Tracy's resentment right now, her unrelenting anger.

She paused and looked behind her for Kara, hidden by some bend in the trail. She waited, sliding the skis back and forth.

Kara appeared a few minutes later, her skiing a little sloppy, as if she were fatigued. "Don't you dare run off until I catch my breath, Danielle," she threatened as she closed the distance between them.

Danny felt remorse. She should have matched her friend's pace. "Sorry. How about some energy?" She slipped off her backpack and removed a bag of dried fruit.

"That's what you call energy?" Kara pulled cookies from her pack and offered one to Danny, who took it with a slight smile.

"I didn't mean to get so far ahead. I was thinking about Tracy. She's been giving me a hard time," Danny said bluntly, feeling somewhat guilty for the admission. Was she ratting on her daughter? "The move's been hard on her."

"I can imagine. My kids are difficult enough and I haven't taken them away from where they want to be. Why did I think I wanted children?" Kara laughed loudly, shattering the white silence. "They were so cute when they were little, but so demanding. They're still demanding but not so cute anymore."

Danny laughed with her. "I asked Tracy to come

4

today, but I don't think she wanted to interrupt her sulk. It's as if she thinks I'm going to change my mind and go back to Craig if she's unpleasant enough." A comfortable silence fell between them while Danny wondered if what she had just said was true. "Well, fuck it all."

"Sounds good to me," Kara said, looking revived. "I've caught my breath but I'm looking for my favorite sign — chalet."

"Let's call it a day then," Danny said reluctantly, hating to leave the trails for the plunge back into reality.

In the lodge, cold, wet clothes, strewn on benches, steamed in the warm air. Puddles of snow melted on the floor. The two women purchased hot chocolate and huddled at a table.

"I think you're brave, Danny. I do. I'd never have the courage to leave Peter." Kara's lovely smooth skin glowed a healthy pink. Her hair sprayed out in a static electric halo.

"It wasn't brave, Kara. I just couldn't stay any longer. I can't even tell you why." Danny ran long, slender fingers through her thick auburn hair, pulling the tangles apart. "Do you want to leave Peter?"

"Not really, I guess."

After dropping Kara off at her large brick house near the golf course, Danny continued to the bottom of the hill on Elm Street, to the home of her youth. Once the street had been lined with graceful elms shaped like wine glasses. They had died years ago, killed by Dutch elm disease, and been replaced with silver maples.

Danny knew that she and Tracy couldn't stay with her mother indefinitely. If Tracy didn't drive her crazy, her mother would. As much as she loved her mother, moving in with her had firmly convinced Danny that the generations should not live together. There was too much friction, too much temptation to play one against another. She pulled into the driveway, parked the blue Ford Escort next to her mother's blue Buick Regal, thinking they looked like mother and child. And that's how she always felt when she returned home, her mother's child.

Her mother's dog, a small barking ball of fury, threw himself against the inside of the door as she pushed it open. She gave the animal a cursory pat, told him to shut his little mouth before she jerked out his little tongue, and stepped into the mud room to remove her boots. Whining for attention, Tipsy followed her into the kitchen.

Her mother stood at the counter in a splash of light streaking through the window over the sink, and Danny knew instantly that something had happened. She recognized the stiff back, the abrupt movements, the failure to turn and smile. Danny sighed involuntarily.

"The skiing must have been good. You were gone long enough."

Danny understood the words to be a rebuke. She hung her jacket in the back closet. "Something wrong, Mom?" she asked.

Charlotte "Charlie" Dennis turned to glare at her.

6

"Your daughter's vocabulary is terrible. It lacks imagination."

So the kid had said *fuck*. When Tracy went into a rage, anything was apt to come out of her mouth. Had she herself been so uncontrollably angry in her youth? "I'm sorry, Mom. I'll talk to her." Danny thought her mother's back relaxed a little. She placed a hand on Charlie's arm, gave it a friendly squeeze. "Okay?"

Charlie nodded.

Heading for the stairs, Danny wondered why her mother hadn't sold this house long ago and either moved into a smaller one or an apartment. Taking care of a house this size was a lot of work — three bedrooms and a bath upstairs, one bedroom, a dining room, living room, kitchen and bath downstairs. Slowly she ascended the threadbare steps, one hand on the bannister to pull herself up. Her body felt heavy, so different than when she was skiing. Depression. The big D, she thought, recalling sessions with her counselor before leaving Craig.

She knocked on Tracy's bedroom door, opened it and peered inside. There in the gloom her daughter lay curled up on the bed with a book. The book was a good sign, denoting interest in something outside herself. It occurred to Danny that the girl might also be depressed.

"May I sit down?" she asked, settling on the double bed without waiting for an answer. She knew Tracy was quite likely to tell her no. She studied her daughter and failed to see the resemblance to herself that everyone was always pointing out.

"Grandma is not ready to hear some of the words you use, Tracy."

"They're all in the dictionary," she replied with shrug.

Danny wanted to shake the girl. "She's right when she says they show a lack of imagination."

"Next time I'll say uck-fay."

In spite of herself, Danny laughed aloud and caught sight of Tracy's lips curving up at the corners, opening into a smile, revealing straight white teeth. A laugh burbled out of her. Danny stared, amazed at the transformation the smile wrought. "When you smile, you're quite lovely, do you know that?"

"Oh, Mom, you just say that because you're my mother." There was disbelief, even disgust, in her tone.

The girl couldn't even accept a compliment from her, Danny thought, much less criticism.

In bed that night, listening to great horned owls hooting in nocturnal courtship, Danny stared at the ceiling. Tomorrow she had two interviews, and although she wouldn't look her best if she didn't get some sleep, thoughts whirled in her mind like the snow that had swirled around her feet during the day.

Craig had called to talk with Tracy early in the evening, unwittingly stirring up trouble. Tracy had distanced herself afterward, refusing to talk, throwing her dishtowel down and rushing from the kitchen for no apparent reason. And Danny, unwilling to let her behavior go unchallenged, had followed her to her room.

She realized that years ago her marriage had

died of its own accord from a mutual lack of interest. She knew, when she confronted her need for a woman, as much amazed by it as by anything in her life, that she could no longer run from this aspect of herself. But she had been unable to level with Craig. When she had opened her mouth to tell him about Rachel, the words hadn't come. She still couldn't say, *I'm a lesbian.*

She decided she needed to tell someone, to say the words out loud, to see confirmation in someone else's eyes. Kara's? Once she had loved Kara that way, unable to admit it even to herself. There had just been the need to be with Kara, to touch her arm or hand.

Turning on her side, she looked out the frosted window and heard tree branches scraping against the glass. Slipping out from under the covers, she shivered in the cold room. Since she and Tracy had arrived, Danny had dreaded the icy air and floors when leaving her bed during the night or in the morning. Tracy and Charlie had silent skirmishes over temperature: Tracy turning up the thermostat, her grandmother turning it down to save money and energy. Standing at the window, she noticed softly falling snow illumined by the streetlight, blanketing the last layer with a fresh clean cover.

At the Tech the next day Danny confronted her interviewers with confidence. If they didn't want her, she told herself, it was their loss. She felt on firm ground here, certified and experienced in her field.

"Some of your students will be barely literate,"

one of the interviewers said. A dignified woman with slightly graying black hair, her bright, nearly black eyes appeared to miss nothing.

"It was that way at the Tech at Roselawn where I last taught. In fact, nearly all the students were poorly grounded in the English language," Danny explained.

The other interviewers asked her some of the questions she knew they would ask, such as, "Why do you think we should hire you?" To which she replied, "Because I'm well qualified and bring years of experience to the job." And, "What do you see yourself doing a few years from now?" Which she answered, "Teaching. I love to teach." Was that true? Sometimes she hated teaching, especially when she had an uninspired class.

When she got up to leave, she thanked them for the interview and shook hands all around. The woman with the black hair and lively dark eyes leaned across the table to take Danny's hand, her own smaller one disappearing in Danny's clasp. They smiled and something, a sort of current, passed between them — although Danny did not believe in instant attraction. She was certain she had mistaken the woman's friendliness for something more.

Her next interview turned into a disaster. The interviewer unnerved her, his eyes gravitating to the open V of her blouse or her long, crossed legs. Although she had dressed conservatively in a gray suit and white blouse, she felt naked under the man's gaze. When she stood, certain she would never get the job and would refuse to take it if offered, she shook his hand with distaste. He walked her to the door and once outside, she sucked in the frigid air and exhaled him with it.

She planned to meet Kara for lunch at Bon Appetit. Glancing at her watch, she drove swiftly through traffic, her mind on the morning. The restaurant, crowded with business people, smelled of freshly baked bread. Inhaling the scent, she looked over the crowded tables and spied Kara seated by a corner window under hanging ferns.

"You look very nice," Kara remarked, her large blue eyes underlined by dark circles.

It had been those eyes Danny had drowned in during her youth. She used to think they looked into her soul. Now she knew they had only seen her surface. "Are you all right?" Concerned, Danny picked up the menu but did not open it.

"Tired. Had a huge fight with Peter last night, another with Johnny this morning. I have three houses to show later this afternoon." Kara sold real estate. "All I want to do is go home to bed and cry myself to sleep." One corner of her sensuous mouth lifted in a wry smile.

Danny gazed at the mouth, looked into the blue eyes, and smiled not only in response but in relief. She no longer needed anything more than friendship from Kara. "I know what you mean. Tracy and I got into it last night after she talked to her father."

"How did the interviews go?" Kara set her menu down. "I'm going to have a tuna salad. It's such a bore always having to watch my weight, but I get to looking like a seal if I'm not careful."

11

Danny laughed, picturing a seal with Kara's head on it. "The one with the Tech went well, I think. The other was a bust."

Kara leaned her elbows on the small round table and presented Danny with a faint, pleased smile. "It's so good to have you back. Do you know that?"

"You don't think I was running home to Mama?" Danny asked, because that was how she thought people might interpret her return to Edgemont, Wisconsin.

"Hell, no. I think it was the sensible thing to do. Now, what are you going to eat?"

Danny ordered and when she handed the waitress her menu, she noticed her interviewers from the Tech standing in the entryway. "This *is* a small town, isn't it?" She told Kara about the people waiting to be seated. "Do you know the woman with them, the one with the dark hair?"

"Nice hair. Wish mine was like that, instead of this disgusting brown mess. She looks familiar, but I don't know her. Maybe I showed her a house once."

Danny forced her attention back to Kara. "Are you selling lots of houses?"

"Enough. Keeps me in clothes. Bought me my last car. Maybe you should go into real estate with me, Danny. We could open our own business — Brown and Jennings. Sounds like a law firm."

"I'm a terrible salesperson. I always feel compelled to point out the flaws in whatever I have to sell." It was true. She was honest to a fault. However, she'd had no trouble lying to Craig about her whereabouts with Rachel, which reminded her of her decision to confide in Kara. Spooning soup into her mouth, hardly tasting it, she thought how she would phrase this admission of lesbianism. She looked up and met Kara's amused gaze. "What is it?"

"If I didn't know you better, I would think you had some terrible secret to tell me."

"Like what?" Feeling a flush rise up her neck and spread across her face, Danny thought with embarrassment that she was probably the only person in the world who still blushed.

Kara's amusement turned pensive. "There is something you want to tell me, isn't there?"

The waitress set Kara's tuna fish plate in front of her and removed Danny's empty soup bowl, replacing it with a spinach salad.

"I can't," Danny said, intently staring into Kara's blue eyes.

"You can tell me anything, Danny. You should know that."

"I can't tell you this."

"I'll pester you until you do, and besides, if you can't tell me, who can you tell?"

Good question, Danny thought, watching Kara's eyes narrow. "No one." She forgot the other people in the restaurant.

"You killed him," Kara hissed, her head snaking forward.

"Killed who?" Danny asked, knowing who. Kara's imagination was vivid and sometimes outrageous.

"Craig. He probably deserved it. Was he cheating?"

"We were both cheating," she admitted.

"Really? Tell me." Kara took a bite of tuna.

Now she should say it, that she had been

cheating with a woman, but suddenly she felt tired. Thinking about her life with Craig made her want to sleep.

"You know what Peter and I fought about last night?"

Danny tried to show interest. The tiredness ebbed.

"I wanted to talk. He wanted to read. Then I wanted to screw and he wanted to watch the tube. I feel cheated if I don't get some sex at least once a week. I don't know why. I followed him around the house, screaming like a shrew. I would have hit me." She looked brightly at Danny, who thought the brightness covered tears.

Danny placed a hand over Kara's and smiled sadly. "I know what you're talking about. I used to do that too until I didn't care anymore."

"And then this morning there was Johnny with his nose in his cereal, looking like his dad, and I hollered at him. Fortunately for her, Laura was spending the night at a friend's house."

"We all do that, Kara. My mother was mad, so I took it out on Tracy."

"I know what you're afraid to tell me," Kara suddenly whispered, amusement lighting up her face. "You're gay."

Danny froze in her chair. The heat returned to her cheeks.

"Oh, God." Kara covered her mouth in a rare exhibit of short-lived surprise. Then she said, "Of course. I should have known." Her voice softened. "It's okay, sweetie. Really. I love you."

"I could be straight and you'd still love me," Danny couldn't resist saying.

14

"True." Kara looked mystified. "But this is infinitely more interesting."

Danny shifted uncomfortably in her chair and glanced around the room.

Kara leaned forward and said in a low voice, "Who were you attracted to in high school?"

Danny suddenly grinned. "You. That's what you wanted to hear, right?"

Kara's face beamed. "I think I knew."

"I'm not anymore, though. So don't worry."

"Who's worried?"

II

The wind ruffled Danny's long hair, lifting the curls off her neck. Just a hint of cold rode in the breeze, a reminder that winter could return the next hour or not at all. A little bit of green brightened yellow willow branches; new grass sprouted in sheltered clumps; scattered patches of early wildflowers colored the woods; buds swelled on the branches of bushes and trees. In a small pond far below her, water moved and sparkled in the sun.

A month ago she had climbed this ridge on cross-country skis with Kara for company. Yesterday morning she had gone to the airport with Kara, who was off to Florida to visit her mother and escape the unrelenting winter.

But spring in Wisconsin excited Danny as only this time of year could.

For weeks Kara had been urging Danny to fly to Florida with her. Before boarding the plane, she had said wistfully, "We'd have such a good time, Danny."

"I can't afford to go. You know that, Kara."

"I told you I'll pay your way. It's worth it to me."

"Oh, Kara, is it so awful to visit your mother alone?"

Resigned, Kara had suddenly smiled. Already a rosy brown from hours in the tanning room at the beauty shop, her smooth skin glowed, the blueness of her eyes a bright contrast. "No, I like my mother. It would just be more fun if you were there too."

"Besides, I have to work." Danny had taken a job at the Ace hardware store in town. Next fall she would start teaching at the Tech, but she had to have income now. Craig's checks came faithfully every week, reproachful reminders of his role as husband and father, but they weren't large enough to pay for more than the necessities — food, clothes, utilities.

Danny was enough of a realist to know that there would not be enough money to move herself and Tracy to a separate residence until the job at the Tech became a reality, or until the house she and Craig owned sold. Living with her mother had become less abrasive with the passing weeks. Routine got them through the days.

Tracy continued to remind Danny of her displeasure at being forced to leave Roselawn High in the middle of her junior year. Still, the phone rang more for Tracy than it did for anyone else in the household. Charlie complained about not being able to talk to her friends, and Danny felt compelled to point out how little time Charlie had spent on the phone before Tracy began monopolizing it.

"Would you rather she had no friends?" Danny had asked her mother that morning, exasperated at having to go through this conversation every day and sometimes more often.

"Of course not. She just doesn't have to hog the telephone. There might be an emergency and how would we know?"

"Come on, Mom." Danny put an arm around her mother's shoulders and squeezed. The woman felt tiny to her, fragile. Was it the nature of mothers and daughters to disagree? Because the pattern repeated itself in Tracy. The three of them verbally sparred — vain attempts to wrest from one another identification, independence, respect. "I'll talk to her, Mom. Maybe she is on the phone too much."

Sunshine lit the kitchen counters and floors, bringing the yellow out of the beige. The two women, warmed by the brightness washing over them, poured coffee and sat at the maple table to read the newspaper. Companionable silence fell between them. Tipsy, who followed Charlie faithfully from room to room, lay in a splash of sun, four legs turned toward the ceiling, snoring softly. The radio, tuned to National Public Radio, quietly played Brahms' *Variations On A Theme By Haydn*. A rare peace had descended over Danny, wrapping her in contentment.

In the afternoon she had fled the house, needing

the nourishment of fresh air, unable to spend a whole day voluntarily indoors. She had left Charlie messing around in the kitchen, Tracy having already gone with the friends she claimed she didn't have. Tipsy appeared at the top of the hill, backtracking, a question in his large brown eyes, his grizzled muzzle dirty from snuffling in the muddy ground. She knew he had come in search of her when he missed her presence on the trail. "Okay, Tips, I'm coming." Her own voice startled her. A squirrel set up an angry chatter. Blue jays screamed in the treetops.

Tomorrow she would return to the hardware store, to the bins of nuts and bolts, screws and nails, hand and electrical tools, bird feeders and bags of seed, doorknobs and hinges — the seemingly endless inventory. Sometimes she spent the entire workday stocking shelves. Some days she never left the check-out counter. There were always customers with questions about plumbing or wiring or shelving, with unclear notions about repairing or replacing or building something. She was expected to answer their questions, to fill in the blanks of their ideas. Each day was different; few bored her. She enjoyed going to work, was not looking forward to quitting the hardware store to teach at the Tech. It surprised her, this propensity for clerking. She never would have guessed it.

She had always been somewhat of an intellectual snob, proud of her B.A. and M.A. degrees in English language and literature. As far back as college, she had been certain that someday she would write a book, as soon as the exigencies of school and work didn't rob her of time. She hadn't decided what kind of book, just a well-written work worthy of praise. As soon as she had a few hours, she would start it, maybe even tonight.

She laughed at her dreams of grandeur. The sound caused a fluttering of wings in nearby pine trees; doves rose, whistling with alarm, and flew away. Tipsy's head had completely disappeared in a hole, muffling his bark. "Someday, dogaroo, you're going to meet up with the burrow's owner. You'll be one sorry pooch then." The woofing became more distant as Tipsy wedged his shoulders in the widening hole. "Get out of there, Tips." When the dog persisted in his pursuit, she sat on a log, waiting for him to give up.

When Danny returned home, she carried a protesting Tipsy to the bathroom, passing her mother in the living room on the way, and set him in the tub.

Charlie appeared in the doorway. "Poor baby," she crooned to the small, shivering dog, whose plaintive cries broke into a series of high-pitched whines that ended in a tiny howl — snout turned toward the ceiling, mouth shaped into an O. His brown, curly coat hung in muddied ringlets.

"Poor baby, my ass. I had to drag him out of holes all afternoon." Danny sprayed water over Tipsy, whose howls turned into low growls. "Behave yourself," she said in a no-nonsense voice, and the little dog gave in, becoming the picture of abject misery.

"You got a call this afternoon from a Maureen Murphy," her mother said. "The number's by the phone."

Danny's heart jumped a little, surprising her. The

woman with the black hair and eyes. What on earth could she want? She toweled Tipsy who, when she let go of his tail, bolted for the living room where he rolled and rubbed himself dry while emitting little grunts.

"Think I'll take a shower, Mom, and then call this Maureen," Danny said casually leaning on the door frame, eyeing the dog. "Do you know what she wanted?"

Charlie glanced up and over her glasses from the book she was reading. She sat in a corner of the couch under a pool of light from a floor lamp. The brown hair of her youth had turned mostly gray; her face was wrinkled softly around the eyes and cheeks and mouth, her neck had lost its firmness, and ropy veins ribbed her hands. She looked all of her sixty-four years, and Danny frowned at the specter of her mother's death, shoved the flash of inevitability into a far corner of her mind. "No, she didn't tell me. Does she have something to do with the Tech?"

"She was one of the people who interviewed me." Danny straightened and started to turn away.

"Maybe they want you to start working there."

Danny hoped not, not yet.

Maureen Murphy answered the phone, her voice low-pitched and husky, sexy.

"You called earlier?" Danny's nervousness escaped her on the last word, and the question ended in a near squeak. She covered the mouthpiece and cleared her throat.

"We're having a picnic for faculty and administration in a few weeks. It's usually a fun time. We move it indoors if the weather doesn't cooperate. It would be nice if you would join us. The third Sunday in April at two?"

"Should I bring anything?" Danny's mind leaped ahead to the picnic, to seeing this woman again, to meeting intelligent people, to making a good impression, to stress.

"Just yourself this time. We don't ask the new faculty members to bring anything. How have you been keeping?"

A strange way of asking how are you, Danny thought. Perhaps the woman came from a different part of the country where they said such things. "Good. Well." Which was it? If she reacted this way to simple questions, perhaps she shouldn't go to any get-together where she would be expected to behave intelligently and speak like an English teacher. "How are you?"

"Outside of a little cold, I'm fine.",

"I thought your voice sounded different."

"Does it?" Maureen gave a throaty laugh. "Bring a friend if you like."

"Thank you. Maybe I will." Should she take Kara? It might be better than going alone and risk being on the edges of conversations, excluded from the camaraderie.

Monday Danny awakened to wind dashing snow against the windows. The last week in March was going out like a lion. Shivering, she forced herself to get out of bed as soon as the alarm went off. Otherwise, Tracy would beat her to the shower.

There were two baths but only one shower. The cold wood floors caused her bare feet to ache.

"Want something special for breakfast? Maybe some scrambled eggs or oatmeal?" she asked Tracy when the girl joined her in the kitchen. Tracy wore old jeans and a baggy sweater.

"Naw. I'll just have a piece of toast."

"Don't you want to wear something nicer to school?" Danny said, regretting the words as soon as they were spoken.

"You're not dressed so hot." The sweet face crumpled into a frown.

Danny wore gray slacks, a white shirt, and black and white patterned sweater. "What's the matter with what I have on?"

"You're dressed like an old lady, like Grandma." The girl's smoky, hazel eyes scanned Danny.

Just getting to the hardware store turned into a major project. Six unforecasted inches of heavy, wet snow had fallen during the early morning hours. First she and Tracy cleared the driveway and sidewalk. Tracy made more headway shoveling than Danny did with the snow blower, which she had to restart every few feet. "Goddamn, frigging thing. What good is it to have one of these when it only handles the stuff that's easy to shovel?"

"What, Mom? What'd you say?" Tracy hollered, snow piling up on her curls.

"You want to run this thing?" she yelled, sweating under her winter jacket.

"No, I'll shovel, but it'd be nice to have some help." Tracy grinned and Danny smiled at the rare sight.

The Escort spun its wheels going up the Elm Street hill, forcing Danny to coast to the bottom and back up even farther to get a running start. As the Ford flew over the crest at the top, she saw a car backing out of a driveway a few hundred feet ahead. Without thinking Danny slammed on the brakes, sending her vehicle into a spin.

"Jeezus, Mom, you never brake when it's slippery out." Tracy's voice was pitched high with fear.

The other car pulled back into the safety of its driveway as the Escort spun past and hit the curb on the right side of the street and jolted to a stop. Danny's heart raced, hardly pausing for a solid beat.

"You all right, sweetie?" she asked.

"Heart attack city," Tracy muttered, the color gone from her face. "Next time you want to do donuts, Mom, I'll show you how."

Danny dropped Tracy off at school and proceeded to Morgan's Ace Hardware. The parking lot had been cleared; a four-wheel-drive truck with a snowplow blade was parked in the far corner. Danny let herself into the back door of the old building. The scuffed hardwood floors creaked under her weight. She turned on the lights, which hung on long chains from the high ceiling. Cranking up the heat, she switched on the overhead fans meant to keep some of the warmth down where the employees and customers could benefit from it.

Shelves, filled with innumerable objects, lined the walls and interior of the long store. She wondered if she would ever learn the entire inventory. Recently, the elderly Mr. Morgan had bowed to technology. The contents of the store could be found on the computer at the check-out counter. Before unlocking

24

the front doors, she checked the cash register and found it held enough change to start the day.

"You're the early bird." Mr. Morgan's son, Brad, startled her — coming out of the depths of the store as he did.

"I thought I was the only one here," she said, one hand over her chest. "The lights were off, the doors locked. So that's where the money came from."

"If you turn on lights before time to open, people start pounding on the door." Brad reached the front door where Danny stood, ready to open to the public. Danny had gone to high school with this man, had dated him more than once, had almost lost her virginity to him in the back seat of his father's Cadillac over twenty years ago.

She looked up at him, still thinking him immensely tall. A runner, she knew, with the skinny neck and lean body that went with the obsession. His gaze met hers and he smiled faintly, his pale blue eyes gleaming with humor, crinkling at the corners. She returned the smile. "What do you want me to do?" she asked.

"I'll go out and clean off the sidewalk. You stay here and take care of things." He reached past her and unlocked the door.

The phone rang off the hook — people wanting Brad to plow them out; others wanting to buy or rent snow blowers; businesses wanting salt delivered to melt the ice on their walks. They were sold out of snow shovels within an hour of opening. Customers tromped in trails of snow. It wasn't possible to keep people home even when the roads were impassible. Danny had found that out long ago. It never kept her home.

The door jangled every few minutes and around ten Tracy showed up — her face pink, her wildly curling hair totally out of control, her eyes watering from the wind. "Hi, Mom."

"Why aren't you in school, sweetie?"

"Snow day."

"We should have listened to the radio." Danny leaned on the counter, thinking how young the girl looked. "What have you been doing all this time? Did you walk here?"

"I walked from Kim's house. Can I take the car home?"

"You won't forget to pick me up at five?"

"Of course not."

Around noon the sun came out, the temperature rose into the forties, and the snow melted in earnest, pouring off gutters to join the ground flow toward the sewers.

"Next they'll be coming in for pumps. You'll see," Brad said. "That your daughter who was here earlier?" When Danny nodded, he said, "She looks like you."

"Have you got kids?" she asked him, realizing how little she knew of his present life. High school twenty-one years ago was a lifetime for some people.

The store was temporarily deserted, and he sat on the counter eating his lunch. "Three boys. They live with their mother and come stay with me on weekends. I always wanted a girl."

"Puberty hits girls hard," Danny replied drily, taking the lid off a container of yogurt.

"You still go around with Kara?" Wiping his mouth, he stood and stretched.

Danny nodded. "She's in Florida right now." She

26

missed Kara, her only close friend in town. Hell, her only real friend here.

"We used to have some good times in high school," he said.

She didn't know if he was referring to good times with Kara or herself and hoped the conversation wasn't heading toward a renewal of those times. The door jangled and their heads swung toward the sound.

"I want ten of those thingamabobs and twenty watchmacallits and five doodads," Charlie said, grinning at them. She pulled off her knit cap and her short gray hair stood on end. She wore moon boots, jeans, and a hooded sweatshirt. It occurred to Danny that Charlie was probably viewed as a town character. "Hi, Brad, how you doing?"

"Can't complain a whole lot. How you doing, Charlie?"

"Bored. I've got a strong case of cabin fever."

"Don't we all, Mom."

"Well, you're not cooped up. You're out and about."

"Did Tracy bring you here?"

"I brought myself. How could she bring me here when I haven't seen her all day?"

"She's not home?" Danny felt her blood pressure zoom upward. The girl was running around with the Escort. "How are the roads?"

"Which you want answered first? No, she's not home, and the roads are pretty good. Spring's back."

At five o'clock Tracy walked into the store. "You ready, Mom?"

Frowning in disapproval, Danny pulled on her jacket.

"What's wrong, Mom?"

"You didn't go home with the car." Danny looked briefly into her daughter's gold-flecked eyes before walking out the door with her. She held out her hand for the keys and Tracy dropped them into her mother's open palm. "Well?" Climbing into the driver's seat, she turned toward the girl.

"I went to Kim's. Is that a crime or something?"

"You could have told someone." Danny started the engine and glanced at the fuel gauge. She couldn't remember how full it had been that morning.

"How did you know anyway? You checking up on me?"

She wouldn't let Tracy put her on the defensive. "Your grandma was in the store around noon."

"She checking up on me now?"

"No. But from what she said I knew she hadn't seen you. Forget it. Just so you weren't driving around. So, tell me about Kim. Why don't you bring her over?"

"She lives in this really big house. Her parents aren't always nosing around," Tracy said, triggering Danny's alarm system.

"Don't they care?"

"They trust her is all." Tracy looked out the window.

A few piles of snow were all that were left of last night's storm. The temperature on the bank sign read fifty-two degrees. Danny rolled her window halfway down and heard the birds singing, saw a few forsythias bravely blooming, smelled spring on the fresh air.

"I trust you, Tracy. It's just that sometimes you're almost secretive." Had she been that way at

Tracy's age? She couldn't remember. What she did remember was Charlie waiting up for her nights, her bathrobe wrapped around her with crossed arms.

In bed that night Rachel walked into Danny's mind, slipped between her thoughts. There she stood — fair hair, gray eyes — looking nothing like her name. Danny reached out in memory and touched the soft skin, listened carefully for Rachel's voice but couldn't hear it until suddenly, clearly, as if Rachel were in the room: "Danny, you don't mean it."

Danny's eyes opened and she noted her surroundings: her childhood room in her mother's house. They had always met at Rachel's apartment with the brightly colored abstracts on the white walls, the off-white carpeting and furniture. Even when there was no sun, those rooms stayed light and airy — like Rachel. Rachel kept unpleasantness at arm's length. She walked away from arguments and obligations. The only commitment she made was to her writing.

Danny had met her at the feminist bookstore during a book signing. She had bought one of Rachel's books, a slim volume of short stories, and stood in line for her autograph. Rachel handed her back the book with a brilliant smile, and Danny fell in love.

She pursued Rachel unrelentingly, chasing an idea as much as a person. With no thought of the consequences, she set after Rachel with a single-mindedness that brooked no refusal. In the end it was absurdly easy to get into Rachel's bed; the difficulty lay in keeping others out of it. She promised to leave Craig for Rachel, but Rachel wanted no permanent bonds. When Danny finally realized there could be no relationship with Rachel and found the strength to walk away, those were her words: "Danny, you don't mean it." Danny had left Craig and run from him as well as from Rachel. There had been no future for her with either of them.

She closed her eyes and felt Rachel's hands on her. Feather soft and hesitant, they moved over the curves and planes of Danny's body. Rachel's mouth, full and warm, followed her hands — lips kissing, tongue tasting. Danny's fingers stole between her legs.

III

"So, how was Florida?" Smiling at the sound of Kara's voice on the phone, Danny added, "I missed you."

"Wonderfully warm and I missed you too. How about we get together Sunday afternoon? Make the day interesting."

"Sure. I wondered if you would come with me to a faculty get-together in a couple weeks? They said I could invite a friend."

"You don't want to go alone and stand in corners.

31

Am I right? Give me the date. I'll put it on my calendar."

Tipsy and Danny met Kara at the door Sunday. The dog's barking drowned their greetings. When Danny hugged her friend, Tipsy nipped Kara's jeans. Danny scolded him into submission. "I'm sorry. Sometimes I think he's barked his brains out."

Kara eyed the animal warily. "He's kind of cute. I don't remember him."

"Mom's had him for years now."

"Where is everyone?"

"Mom's playing bridge. Tracy's gone with the friends she claims she doesn't have." Danny spread her arms wide. "We've got the place to ourselves, and since it's raining buckets out, why don't we stay here?"

Kara shed her raincoat and shook water from her head. "Sounds good. The kids and their friends were driving me up one wall and down another. Loud music, shouting. Peter is holding down the fort." She took the davenport, stretching her arms across the back.

Danny sat in a reclining chair nearby. "Tell me about your vacation."

"I spent my days by the pool or walking the beaches. You would have loved it."

"How's your mother?"

Frowning, Kara chewed on her lower lip. "Slipped some since I last saw her. A little slower, you know? Forgetful, gets tired quicker, talks less." She shrugged and sighed. "How's Charlie?"

"I looked at her the other day and noticed how she's aged. It scared me."

Kara patted the cushion next to her. "Sit next to me, will you?"

Smiling slightly, Danny moved near her friend. "Why?"

"You just seemed kind of far away." Kara's arm slipped around Danny's shoulders, no easy feat since Danny was taller by several inches. "Danny?"

"What?" Danny looked into the blue eyes and felt her pulse jump. "No, Kara." She shook her head.

"How do you know what I'm going to say before I say it? Hmm?" Kara looked amused. Very tan, she glowed with color.

"It could ruin a beautiful friendship." Why did she want to laugh, Danny wondered.

"Just once. Please."

"You just want to know what it's like, don't you?"

"I do," Kara admitted eagerly. "And I love you."

"Not that way you don't." Danny studied the blue depths. Desire stirred. It had been months since she'd had any sex with anyone other than herself.

"Come on." Kara stood and tugged at Danny's hand.

What if her mother returned early? What if Tracy came home? These thoughts tumbled through Danny's mind, leaving behind possible explanations for different scenarios. *We were just listening to music, Mom.* Or, *I was showing Kara a book.* Did she need to offer excuses at her age?

Danny closed and locked the bedroom door behind them. She momentarily leaned against it, watching Kara walk around the room. Then, switching the bedside radio to National Public Radio, she let a Bach violin concerto into the room.

"Nice," Kara said, turning toward Danny, smiling nervously.

"We can just talk, you know, like we used to on Sunday afternoons. Remember?"

"It's hot." Kara shed her sweater. Her hair flew away from her head, causing that electric halo.

Danny's gaze fell to the soft breasts outlined by a clinging blouse, then rose to Kara's flushed face and too-bright eyes. She laughed a little. "Kara, you don't want to do this."

"Yes, I do," Kara said firmly, moving close to Danny and looking expectantly into her face.

Backing away, Danny sat on the bed and took her friend's hands. "You've got to promise we'll still be friends afterward."

"Yes, I promise."

Lust danced between them. Danny saw it in Kara's eyes, a glazed look. She reached for her, pulling the shorter woman onto the bed. "Let's just lie here for a while." Wrapping her arms around Kara, she felt the soft curves against her leaner body. "You smell good. You always smelled good. Nearly drove me crazy when we were young."

"Did it?" Kara's voice sounded throaty. Her mouth met Danny's and she murmured, "If I'd only known, maybe this would have happened years ago."

"Oh, Kara, you spent your youth chasing boys." Danny kissed the full warm lips, tasted them.

"What a waste." Kara threw an arm over Danny, holding her close.

Danny ran a caressing hand over her friend, unbuttoned her blouse, unsnapped her bra, and molded the freed breasts with her hands. The nipples hardened under her fingers.

Back arching, Kara whispered into Danny's mouth, "What's that?"

The scratching at the door, at first only a negligible sound, now resembled frantic digging.

Danny lifted her head. "Tipsy, damn you. Stop it."

"Danny? You upstairs?" Charlie's voice broke into their passion, throwing buckets of icy water on it.

The two women sprang apart and leaped guiltily to their feet. Kara fastened her bra, buttoned her blouse with trembling, awkward fingers. Danny straightened her clothes and ran her fingers through her own thick auburn hair and then smoothed Kara's. Kara's eyes were two large, frightened, blue orbs.

Danny smiled reassuringly. "Mom would never think of such a thing, you know."

Tucking her blouse into her pants, Kara replied softly, "What a rude shock. Can we go somewhere else?"

Danny unlocked the door and they stepped into the hall. At the sound of Charlie's voice, the dog had stopped his efforts to dig a hole through the door. Motioning Kara to lead the way with a hand on her back, Danny followed her downstairs. She sucked in air with each step. After the initial shock of discovery wore off, she found the desire still there. Watching Kara's backside move, she longed to touch it.

"Well, I wondered who was visiting," Charlie said when Kara and Danny sidled into the living room. "How are you anyway, Kara?"

"Good, Charlie. And you? How was bridge?" Kara's face brightened with a smile.

"I'm fine. We snatched a couple rubbers from the opposition. What are you two up to?"

An innocent question, Danny thought after carefully examining her mother's face. She glanced at Kara, whose smile stretched into an enormous grin, whose eyes danced with mischief. "We're just going for a ride."

"It's pouring out."

Danny shrugged. "I like riding in the rain." She smiled at Kara.

"So, where to?" Danny asked once they closed the doors on Kara's Pontiac.

"I want to finish what we started," Kara said in a thick voice.

"How? We can't park and neck."

"Motel room?"

"We'd have to go out of town."

"Let's." The engine purred to life.

But they didn't. Instead, they drove to the mall and threaded their way through the human traffic.

"Next time," Kara suggested when she took Danny home. Danny jumped out of the car and shot into the side door.

Tracy looked up from the counter where she and Charlie were rolling dough. "Hi, Mom."

"This girl doesn't know how to cook," Charlie said.

It sounded like an accusation to Danny. "She never wanted to learn." Danny bent to run a hand over Tipsy's small head.

"We're making pies. Where you been, Mom?"

Shrugging out of her slicker, Danny hung it to dry in the mud room. "Out with Kara. Where did you go?"

"Out with Kim. Her parents bought her a car for her birthday."

Goody, Danny thought wryly, something else to worry about. She lingered for a few minutes in the warmth of the kitchen, pouring herself a cup of coffee and putting it to heat in the microwave. In the living room, she curled up in one corner of the couch and listened to the rise and fall of their voices. Rain continued to splash against the windows. Warm light from the old-fashioned, standing lamp bathed the ancient davenport, which had grown up with Danny. Paging through the Sunday paper, she felt cozy, almost privileged, protected from the elements.

Kara and Danny arrived at the faculty party a few minutes early. A tent had been erected on the Tech campus and under it tables stood laden with food. The two women honed in on the bar, set up at one end of the buffet. They carried small plastic wine glasses to a far corner of the tent.

"Shouldn't you mingle?" Kara asked.

Danny shifted uncomfortably. "I don't know anyone."

"Well, how are you going to get to know anyone standing here with me?"

Danny glanced at her friend. "You come with me and we'll circulate."

They approached two women and a man, introduced themselves, answered a few questions, listened to the conversation and moved on. Someone tapped Danny on the shoulder.

"Danielle Jennings?" Maureen Murphy had apparently been trying to close in on them.

"Call me Danny. Please." She extended a hand for the woman to shake and then placed that hand on Kara's back and introduced her.

"Have you two met anyone?"

Many more people had arrived and the crowd spilled from under the tent onto the lawn, the noise of conversation swelling with the numbers.

"A few, three to be exact."

"Let me take you both around." Sunglasses covered the dark eyes. Maureen's hair floated around her head much like Kara's did.

Danny allowed Maureen to take her arm as they walked, and she studied the delicate features when Maureen leaned in front of Danny to talk to Kara.

"You look so familiar."

"I sell real estate. I swear I've met you too."

"I was looking at houses a year ago. Maybe you showed me one or two."

"Did you buy anything?"

"No, I had a falling out with my financial partner."

"Well, if you ever decide to look again, I'd love to help you."

"Good. That's not my bailiwick."

As she admired the soft curve of jaw, the high cheekbones, the alabaster skin, Danny's interest in this woman, already kindled, caught fire.

"First I want you to meet Michael Lamers. You'll like him."

Michael stood outside the tent, devouring a plateful of hors d'oeuvres. He stood a slightly cadaverous six-plus feet tall. The sun set his red hair aflame, while his green eyes glowed out of sunburned skin. "Ladies, where are your plates? This stuff is too good to pass up. Best herring I ever ate."

Maureen introduced Danny and Kara.

"Now who's who here? Who's teaching English?" he asked, mopping his chin with a napkin.

"I am," Danny replied with a slight smile.

"I have a question. Is it, 'Hopefully I'll get the job,' or 'I am hopeful about getting the job,' or 'I'll get a hopeful job?' "

Danny laughed. "The middle one is okay. The last one doesn't make much sense, and the first is hopefully misused — as it usually is," she added, knowing he was having fun with her.

"Thank you. I know you'll come in handy. I teach word processing. And you sell houses?" he asked Kara.

Kara nodded.

"What's the price of that white elephant on Grove Street?"

"You're interested?" Kara eyed him with her own brand of hope.

"My roommate and I are looking. We'd like to open a bed and breakfast."

"Wonderful idea for that house. But I don't know the price offhand. I do know which one you're talking about, though." She looked thoughtful. "I can find out and call you."

"Would you?" he said enthusiastically. "But now let's move to the tables and fill our plates." The three women trailed after him as if he were the Pied Piper.

"What do you do besides interviews?" Danny, walking backward, asked Maureen.

"I'm in charge of personnel."

One of the tent posts hit Danny between the shoulder blades. Face on fire, she turned and stumbled on the uneven ground. Kara caught her arm, steadying her. Humiliated, she laughed a little.

"Careful," Michael said cheerfully. "That ground can be treacherous. Reaches up and trips you."

After eating, Maureen offered to introduce Danny to the staff with whom she'd be working. Kara stayed with Michael. Danny heard their intermittent laughter as she made idle chatter with other faculty members.

"They're having a good time, aren't they?" Maureen commented as she and Danny broke away from one group and headed toward another.

Heart pounding in her throat, Danny asked, "Would you like to go out some night? Maybe to a movie or something?"

Maureen, who had removed her sunglasses, gave Danny a friendly look out of indecipherable black eyes, smiled wryly and said, "Sure. Give me a call."

On the way home Danny told Kara. "I asked her if she'd like to go out some night."

"Maureen?" Kara inquired, lifting her arched eyebrows even higher. "What about us?"

Danny frowned. "There is no us, Kara, except as friends. You're married."

"Can't we just do it once?"

"We tried," Danny reminded her.

"Let's try again."

Remembering the feel of Kara, Danny relented a little. "Maybe, when it seems right." She turned the Escort into Kara's driveway and parked behind her Grand Am.

"Why don't you come in? You haven't seen Peter and the kids in ages, have you?"

The house greeted them with silence. They walked through the rooms to the staircase. Kara called up the steps, "Anyone home?" When there was no answer, she said, "Come on. I'll show you the house."

Following Kara up the carpeted staircase, Danny wondered if Kara intended to seduce her in a bedroom. But, startling them both, a girl who Danny could only assume was Laura met them in the upstairs hallway. Behind the girl, who looked at them out of huge, blue, scared eyes — Kara's eyes, Danny thought — loomed a skinny, frightened boy. She thought of herself and Kara confronting Charlie after their brief passion.

"What's going on, Laura?" Kara asked sharply. "What are you two doing up here?"

"Nothing," Laura said quickly. "We just came up to get something."

"It doesn't look like you found it," Kara said.

"I'm just now going to look."

"I think you can look without Steve."

The boy, edging past Kara and Danny and mumbling a few words, fled down the stairs.

Kara marched into Laura's room on her daughter's heels. "Why was he up here?"

Danny left them alone and slipped outside, closing the door quietly behind her. It could just as easily have been Tracy, she knew. Starting the Ford's engine, she pondered the situation. What was a mother to do? The car coasted down the hill to Elm Street. She could urge her daughter to use birth control. Or she could suggest that she

41

masturbate or do it with another girl to avoid pregnancy. A smile curled Danny's lips as she parked next to her mother's car.

The sun, hanging low in the west, cast shades of red across the horizon and colored the clouds elsewhere in pink tones. New leaves appeared translucent in the fading light. The muted sounds of birds settling down for the coming night reached her ears. She relished these telltale signs of spring.

Charlie held the phone out for her when she entered the house. "For you. Kara."

"Thanks, Mom." She pressed the receiver to her ear.

"Why did you leave?" Kara demanded.

"It looked like you had your hands full."

"Do you think they're doing it?" Kara sounded bleak.

"I don't know. If they're not, they're sure thinking about it."

"I'm getting the girl some birth control. Do you think I should?"

"Yes. I think I'll do the same with Tracy."

"You don't think that'll look like I'm giving my stamp of approval, do you?"

"No. You can let her know you don't think it's a good idea." Danny glanced at her mother, who was within hearing. She turned her back.

"What a way to end a nice afternoon, huh? By the way, thanks for asking me along. I had a good time."

"You and Michael sounded like you were having fun."

"He's queer as cat shit, isn't he? Why are gay men so much fun?"

"I don't know enough gay men to answer that. Do you?"

"Maybe not. I meant what I said about us, Danny. I'm a little jealous of Maureen, you know."

Danny didn't know what to do with that. "You have your life. I have to make one for myself." She lowered her voice even more. "Kara, you have to help me with this."

"I'm not sure I can. Can you talk?"

"Not really."

"Okay, I'll let you go. Talk to you later."

"Well, how was the party?" Charlie asked as Danny hung up.

"Fun. Interesting. Good food. Where's Tracy?"

"Out somewhere. I can't keep tabs on the girl."

"Think I'll take Tipsy for a walk. It's such a nice evening." Wanting to think, to be alone, Danny turned to the dog who danced excited circles as soon as the leash appeared. "Hold still," she said.

They walked the block to the park, and Danny sat on a bench while the setting sun spread a blush over the river. A soft breeze lifted the heavy hair from her forehead and neck. She smelled the heady scents of water and earth and listened to the sounds of life around her: the ducks and geese muttering from the water, two squirrels chirring, a cardinal's repetitive singing. Tipsy lay at her feet.

"What's he eating, Mom?"

Danny jumped and turned to face her daughter, who had walked up behind her. "Sit down." She patted the bench and moved over to make room. "Grass. It does something for his digestive system," she explained, looking into the heart-shaped face and smiling.

"Grandma said you might be here. Spring drives me crazy."

"Me too. How does it do it to you?" She watched Tracy stretch her legs and stuff her hands into her jeans' pockets. The girl looked so slender, so fragile. There hardly seemed enough flesh and bone.

"Makes me want something without knowing what it even is I want. You know?"

"Yep. I know. It makes me yearn and I don't know what for either. I can hardly stand to be indoors. I keep looking for something or someone."

"Really?" Tracy asked, eyeing her mother with interest.

"Really. We need to talk, sweetie."

"Uh oh." Tracy sat up straight. "What about?" she asked warily.

"About birth control." Danny glanced at her daughter, observed the flush move over her skin.

"You think I'm doing it," the girl accused belligerently. "You don't trust me."

"It's not a matter of trust. It happens even with the best of intentions. I know." Warming to the subject, she continued, "I don't think it's a good idea for you to be sexually active. Sex is just too intensely personal to be taken lightly. But I think you should be prepared just in case."

"Did you have to get married, Mom?" Shadows hid Tracy's expression.

Danny paused for thought, then spoke quietly. "I was pregnant, if that's what you mean."

"You didn't want me, did you?"

"Oh, I wanted you." There was no way she could explain those complicated and sometimes conflicting feelings.

"So that's why you married Dad."

"I was in love with your dad." And she had been in love with him at first, for years.

"You don't love him now," Tracy said sadly.

Danny reached for her daughter's hand. "I still love him, but I'm not in love with him — no. I love you very much." The river flowed past, lit only by the darkening sky and the lights from shore. Its restlessness stirred Danny's. She shifted on the hard seat and squeezed Tracy's hand.

IV

Danny leaned on the counter Monday, watching
the play of light through the windows Brad was
washing. The rays, zeroing in on the glass, created a
miniature sun so dazzling Danny narrowed her eyes
against it. The floorboards radiated warmth.

She considered calling Maureen tonight. There
was a movie she wanted to see at the downtown
theater. Perhaps the two of them could go to dinner
first. A date. Was she right about Maureen? Maybe

she should first check with Michael. Kara had his number.

The bell jangled as the door opened and the first four customers of the day walked in. The smells of April clung to their clothes. "May I help you?" Danny asked.

Just after noon Kara swooped into the store like the homecoming queen she had been in high school. From behind the check-out counter, Danny admired the beautifully tailored linen suit. "Chic outfit."

Kara smiled wickedly. "Thanks, sweetie. I'd take it off for you."

Glancing quickly around for eavesdroppers, Danny hissed, "Someone might hear."

Kara leaned across the counter and whispered back. "How about tonight? The kids will be gone and Peter has Lion's Club."

"For God's sake, give it a rest." But she couldn't stop a grin.

"Then let's go out to eat instead. I'll pick you up after work."

Before Danny could reply, Kara left the store, her heels beating a tattoo on the uneven wood floors. Danny watched her go, thinking Kara always gave the appearance of having everything under control. She had forgotten to ask for Michael's number.

Danny climbed into Kara's car that evening and leaned back against the seat. As the breeze through the open window tugged softly at her hair, she shut her eyes and breathed deeply.

"Where do you want to eat?" Kara asked.

"You choose."

Placing a hand on Danny's leg, she suggested, "Room service."

Tensing, Danny opened her eyes and met Kara's blue gaze. After a brief pause, she relented. "All right. I give in."

"Hot damn," Kara exclaimed, beaming, and Danny laughed.

One lamp shed shadowed light over the motel room. Danny gazed at Kara's lush body. She ran a hand over the golden skin, the generous breasts, the slight swell of belly and cupped the damp curls between Kara's legs before burying her fingers in the tangle. "You're wet clear through," she whispered, Kara's excitement fueling her own. Bending, she took a dark nipple to suckle.

Kara moaned and raised her hips. "Oh, Danny, that feels so good."

Slowly, gently, she coaxed Kara into a frenzy of movement and sound. Danny, whose previous sexual partners had been relatively quiet during the act of love, became somewhat alarmed at Kara's noisy exuberance.

Afterward, when Kara reached for her, Danny murmured, "Lie still. Enjoy it."

Visually exploring the dim, impersonal room, Danny let her mind drift on a wave. As a youth, she had desperately wanted just to touch Kara's lovely skin, and now these many years later, she had been permitted — no, begged — to do just that. Her hand moved idly over the soft, smooth body next to her. She tasted again the warm breast nearest her mouth, then asked, "Well, how was it?"

Kara pulled Danny up next to her and looked into her eyes. "Ecstatic. I didn't want it to end."

"Good. That's the way it should be."

Rolling onto her back, Danny closed her eyes and allowed Kara's touch. She tried. They tried. But finally she hugged Kara, kissed the bluish eyelids and full mouth and said, "It's no use. Maybe we've been friends too long." Then, when Kara looked distressed, added, "It's okay. I enjoyed it."

"Oh, Danny, I want to make you feel as good as you did me. How did you get to be such a wonderful lover anyway?"

In answer, Danny began again — caressing Kara's length with her hands and mouth.

"Don't stop," Kara groaned, her back arched, her fingers clenching Danny's hair.

On the way home through a black, star-strewn night, Danny asked for Michael's number.

"Why do you want it?" Kara asked, tossing over her address book and turning on the map light. She lovingly stroked Danny's bent head.

"I need to ask him something," Danny replied evasively.

When she got home, she took Tipsy for a walk and called Michael from a pay phone in the park. "Do you remember me?" she asked him. "Danny Jennings from the Tech picnic."

"Refresh me."

"Hopefully misused. The new English instructor."

"Oh, yes. The woman with the beautiful eyes and lovely hair and wonderful legs."

"What a nice way to be remembered," Danny responded, pleased.

"Just because I don't want to date you, honey,

doesn't mean I have an unappreciative eye. I need to call your friend about that house on Grove Street. What's her name?"

"Kara Brown."

"That's it. I've got her number here somewhere."

"Are you really thinking about turning that big house into a bed and breakfast?"

"For gays. What do you think of that?"

"The neighbors will love it."

"Well, we don't have to tell the world we're a bunch of queens, but we can discreetly advertise that way. And maybe we'll encourage the ladies of the club to come too."

It would be easy to ask him now, she thought. "Do you know Maureen Murphy very well?"

"She's a good friend. Still hasn't found herself another woman. She's maybe a little too independent." He tsked into the phone, making Danny smile. "You interested in her, sweetie?"

"Well, I wanted to give her a call. Maybe ask her out for dinner or something."

"You should do that. I've got an idea, though. Why don't you come here for dinner next Friday night, and I'll ask Maureen and some other people too? Bring Kara. We'll have a party. Sixish for cocktails sound all right?"

Danny hung up and walked away from the river. A new moon floated in the sky, and the scent of lilacs followed her. She greeted the people she passed, pulling Tipsy against her side. The warm night air felt friendly, promising another nice day tomorrow.

Danny envisioned Kara's tan skin against the white sheets, the dark triangle of hair, the nipples more brown than pink. Trying to pin down her feelings about their sexual encounter, she couldn't get a grasp on it and let it slip away from her. She didn't know what she felt.

"I'll drive," Danny had said when she asked Kara to go with her to Michael's Friday night dinner party. Now, she parked in front of Kara's brick home and walked to the front door. Lights burned behind every window and illuminated the front porch.

The door opened inward and a sturdy boy greeted her.

"You must be Johnny." A safe guess, she thought.

"You must be Danny," he replied with a shy grin.

How old was he? She tried to remember. Around twelve, she believed. He led her to the living room, first calling up the stairs to his mother, and abandoned her. Danny sat in a leather easy chair and picked up the evening paper.

"Hello, Danny." The man standing before her also looked sturdy.

"Peter," she said, extending her hand. She had always liked Peter. He seemed tolerant and tolerable. "I haven't seen you in ages."

"I hear you moved back to town."

It suddenly dawned on her that she had cuckolded this man, and she looked away as if he might read it in her eyes. "Yes. To stay."

He perched across the room on the davenport, resting his arms on his thighs. Running fingers through still plentiful hair, he said, "I hope you two have a good time tonight."

Kara entered the room. "Ready?" she asked Danny as she kissed Peter's forehead.

Danny rose to her feet and started out the door with her. "Do you know where Buchanan Road is?"

"Sure. I'll get us there," Kara promised.

Michael met them at the door of his condominium and welcomed them into his home with a sweep of his arm.

Beige carpeting and furniture, off-white walls with brightly colored prints reminded Danny of Rachel's apartment. She experienced a moment of intense pain.

"What can I get you to drink?" he asked, baring small, straight teeth in a grin. "You're the first ones here."

"Who's coming?" Danny asked.

"My other half, Tony Copinski. He's just not home yet. And Maureen. She's probably the only one you know. Kevin Thomas and Mark Hastings. And Chris Bauman. You'll like her."

"Nice place, Michael," Danny remarked.

"Thanks, but I want a home that isn't identical to all the others around it. Sometimes I have trouble finding my own door."

"I brought the print-out for the house on Grove Street." Kara handed him a sheet of paper and he laid it on the counter to read.

"Listen to this: six bedrooms, four and a half baths, a huge living room, a formal dining room, an immense kitchen, a sunroom and an open porch, a three-car garage with a small apartment above it out back, an acre and a half of lawn. Sounds splendid, don't you think?" he said with enthusiasm. "I can't wait to show this to Tony."

Michael's gangling appearance belied the grace with which he moved to answer the ringing doorbell. Danny heard him ask, "You two girls come together?"

Her heart plunged. Was Maureen with someone? She got off the bar stool and stood next to Kara near the fireplace.

Extending her hand, Maureen covered the short distance to Danny and Kara. "Good to see you two again." Her dark eyes flashed with humor. "Chris and I met on the doorstep."

About Kara's height, Chris was in her mid- to late thirties, with blondish hair curling around her face. She looked fit and athletic. And Danny would have thought she was gay had she met her anywhere, which caused her to wonder why. Was it the hair, the clothes, the stance? Did she herself appear gay to others? She shrugged the unanswerable questions away.

Next to arrive were Mark and Kevin, both dark and short and good-looking. They looked more like brothers than lovers. Tony let himself in as they all sat in the living room, discussing the large house on Grove Street. He joined the talk after saying hello to the guests. As tall as Michael, with exaggerated facial features — large, wide-set, dark eyes, a big nose, a fleshy mouth, enormous ears — he gave the impression of being oversized. When he laughed, his mouth stretched so that his face looked larger than life, a caricature.

Danny studied his huge hands and wondered if the saying, "large hands, large penis," had any truth to it. She glanced at Kara, who was also looking at his hands, and read her thoughts. Their eyes met and Kara made a face. Danny laughed and looked away.

Dinner was pizza and salad. "I didn't have time to do anything else," Michael said, setting the food on TV trays. "Just stay put. We'll eat here in the living room." He filled wine glasses and passed them around.

Balancing a paper plate topped with pizza and a glass of Rhine wine, Danny inched her way along the soft carpeting until she was near Maureen. From a cross-legged position on the floor she peered up at Maureen, who sat in a low-slung, leather chair looking down at her. Michael had closed the blinds and the artificial lighting softened Maureen's smile. Danny asked, "When do classes end at the Tech?"

"There are some summer courses."

"Do you get a vacation?"

"Oh, yes. Three weeks. I didn't know what to do with them last year." The dark eyes turned darker and the lights dancing in them momentarily went out. Maureen clasped her knees and gave Danny the slightest hint of a smile. "What would you do with vacation time?"

Danny, staring at the dark eyes and small red mouth, nearly missed the question. She belatedly answered, "Camp or ski, depending on the season."

Maureen commented, "You look like the outdoorsy type."

Kara spoke from across the room. "When we go cross-country skiing, I'm lucky if I see her backside."

Maureen looked amused. "I'd just as soon sit inside by the fire and read a book."

"I love to ski," Chris put in.

"I'll bet you're good, too," Kara said, eyeing Chris's trim figure.

"So, what do you think of this place?" Michael asked, waving the print-out. He sprawled at the edge of the circle, Tony propped against his chest. He wrapped long arms around Tony, who pulled Michael's face down and gave him a loud kiss on the mouth.

"It looks like a wonderful house for a bed and breakfast," Maureen answered. "I wish you luck."

On the drive home Danny said, "I don't know how they can afford a down payment on that house, much less mortgage payments or taxes and upkeep."

Kara nodded, her face illuminated every hundred feet or so by streetlights. "Interesting people. So different from the parties I go to where the women often sit in one group, the men in another." She turned toward Danny. "Did you make a date?"

"Not yet. I will, though." Danny glanced at her. "I feel like I belong with these people, that they understand my needs better, maybe have some of the same priorities."

"And you don't have to hide your sexual identity," Kara added quietly.

"That too."

When Danny got home, she found a note on the door. Charlie had gone to the hospital emergency room. Tracy had been in an accident. Leaping back in the car, Danny drove in terror to Mercy Medical, running yellow lights and traveling up to forty miles per hour on the city streets.

Charlie sat in the waiting room. Braced for bad news, Danny said, "Tell me, Mom." Why hadn't she left a number where she could be reached?

In the harsh hospital lights Charlie again looked more than her age. Her soft, loose skin sagged, pulling down the corners of her eyes and mouth. She wore a pink sweat suit. "There was a little accident. I got a call an hour or so ago. I didn't know where you were."

Danny hurried to the desk and inquired, "My daughter, Tracy Jennings? I'd like to see her." She turned to look at Charlie, who stood just behind her. "What kind of accident?"

"Her friend Kim's car. I think it went into a ditch."

"Mrs. Jennings?"

Danny turned and met the cool gaze of a policeman. "Yes?"

"Your daughter's all right."

"I think I'd rather hear that from a doctor."

"You will. But she'd been drinking."

Just when things started to go right for a change. Danny's fists curled tightly. She fumed, angry with Tracy and wanting to protect her at the same time. She turned back to the person behind the desk. "I want to see her."

The woman got up and led her through the swinging doors to a nursing station.

Danny knew that Charlie and the policeman were on her heels. She started to tell her mother that she wanted to see Tracy alone, then caught sight of the worry on Charlie's face. Grasping her soft hand, she squeezed it before leaving her mother in the hall.

Tracy, a gauze pad taped to her forehead, looked up at Danny from the high bed in one of the emergency rooms. The flesh around her eyes was darkening and her pupils were so dilated they nearly blocked out the color. "Hi, Mom."

Danny's eyes traveled the length of her daughter's body, searching for damage. Other than the bruised head and eyes and some scratches on her arms, the girl looked unhurt.

A young doctor smiled reassuringly at her from across the bed. "We just got her back from X ray. No broken bones. Her head's banged up but there's no apparent concussion. Just in case, though, she should be kept quiet for a few days." He touched Tracy's arm. "You're a lucky young lady."

"How is Kim?" Tracy asked, sounding small and unsure of herself.

"She was thrown from the car. She does have a concussion and a broken arm, but she's fortunate too." He turned to Danny. "You can take her home, Mrs. Jennings."

"Thanks." Danny watched the white back disappear through the door before saying, "A policeman is waiting out there with Grandma."

"Did she do something wrong?" Tracy raised herself gingerly until she rested on her elbow.

Glaring at the girl, Danny spoke sternly, "This isn't funny, Tracy."

"I know, Mom. I'm sorry I'm such a bother. I want to see Kim. Will you ask if I can see her?"

Why not, Danny thought. She wouldn't mind seeing Kim either, since she had never met her. She asked at the nursing station if it would be possible

57

to see the other girl. Then she returned to Tracy's side and helped her put on her shoes and stand up.

"You okay, sweetie?"

"I'm okay, Mom."

Standing near the door with Charlie, Danny watched Tracy talk to Kim. "How you feeling?" Tracy asked her friend.

Kim's right arm supported a white cast. She was heavier than Tracy, and her long, reddish hair was frizzed in a similar hairdo. The blue of her eyes was nearly blacked out by the size of her pupils.

"It's my head, Trace. It's killing me. Makes me want to puke. They're going to keep me here overnight."

"That's good. I'll talk to you tomorrow." Tracy touched the plaster arm.

"There's a cop here."

"I know. He's waiting for me outside. That's my mom and grandma over there."

Kim waved feebly in Danny and Charlie's direction. "My mother took my dad home. She'll be back." Danny could barely hear her. "They're furious."

"Those two aren't exactly thrilled either," Tracy remarked.

They left Kim and headed to the waiting room, where the policeman suggested they talk. "Where did you get the beer?" he asked Tracy.

With Danny and Charlie flanking her, she defiantly met his eyes with lifted chin. "Took it from Kim's house."

"You might have to appear in juvenile court, you know," he said. "You could be fined. You will be required to go to a drug and alcohol class."

The newspaper had said the county authorities were cracking down on underage drinking, Danny remembered, even punishing first offenders.

"Penance," the girl remarked.

"Show some respect, Tracy," Charlie snapped.

Anxious to get this over, to take Tracy home, Danny rose to her feet.

As they neared the exit, Charlie remarked under her breath, "She's got no respect for authority."

"Oh, Mom," Danny said with exasperation. She glanced at her daughter, who walked in front of them. The kid was running scared, on the defensive, brazening it out. It was what she would have done at Tracy's age. The girl had been brave to insist on seeing her friend, to give Kim her own brand of comfort.

"Didn't you ever do anything wrong when you were young, Grandma?" Tracy turned and grimaced at Charlie.

"I was more discreet."

"That just means you didn't get caught." Tracy's eyes now dominated her face, and she sat down with a thump on a chair by the door.

"I'll get the doctor," Charlie said, turning white herself.

"No. I'm okay. Get the car, Mom. Please." When her mother hesitated, she said, "Honest. I'll be fine."

But before they left they had the doctor take one

last look at Tracy. And there were no more critical words that night. If the girl had planned to frighten her mother and grandmother into silence, she had succeeded, Danny thought as she helped Tracy to bed.

V

Danny fidgeted, wrapping the phone cord around her fingers, moving from one foot to the other. "That would be really nice," Maureen purred in her ear, causing Danny to go weak in the knees. She pictured Maureen's fine-featured, aristocratic face, the dark eyes dancing with lights. She imagined the rosy lips curled upward in a small, amused smile.

Charlie came into the room with the newspaper and plunked herself onto the sofa. Her hair stood up in a gray spray like a dried bouquet of grass, and

61

Danny knew her mother's ears were probably tuned into the conversation.

"Why don't I pick you up at five-thirty? Where do you live?" Danny wrote the address and directions to Maureen's home on the back of an envelope, then said goodbye as Tracy slammed in the back door.

"Hi, Mom. You going somewhere?"

"Your mother's got a Friday night date."

"I'd appreciate it, Mom, if you didn't listen to my phone conversations."

"Who are you going out with?" Tracy asked. She had been subdued since the accident with Kim. Her eyes still looked bruised, and she sported a lump on her forehead.

"It's hard not to hear when you're in the same room with me," Charlie said.

"Why don't you get a phone in your bedroom, Mom?"

"So you can use it, I suppose," Danny remarked dryly.

Tracy shrugged and sat down on the davenport with her grandma. "It'd be nice to have some privacy."

All day Friday Danny watched the clock nervously. Home from work that afternoon, she took the stairs two at a time with Tipsy yapping at her heels, pulled off her clothes and climbed into the shower even before the water warmed. Then she pondered what to wear. Slacks, certainly, but how dressy? Not too, she decided, laying some clothes on the bed. As she dragged underwear over her not-quite-dry bottom, she heard the back door open and close and watched Tipsy jump to his feet to disappear in a rush of frenzied barking. Danny hoped to get out of the house without any discussion about where she was going and with whom, but she met her mother downstairs talking baby-talk to the dog.

Charlie looked up and grinned sheepishly at her daughter, then said, "My, don't you look nice."

"Thanks." Danny opened the back door. "I may be late tonight."

"Have a good time," Charlie called after her.

She appreciated her mother more for respecting her privacy and, for the most part, not interfering in her relationship with Tracy. She herself would try to tread that fine line with Tracy. Reflecting on Tracy, she wondered if she should have let her go out tonight, but she had grounded her for a week. And she thought the girl had been frightened into good behavior. No point in rubbing her nose in it.

Maureen lived on the first floor of a large, old, turn-of-the-century house that had been divided into apartments in which everything was big, tall, and ornate — the windows and doors, the ceilings, the woodwork. The spaciousness made Danny feel a little lost. Braided rugs offered a bright contrast to hardwood floors. Comfortable furniture was interspersed with obvious antiques — a tall, dark secretary, a pine Hoosier cupboard, a solid oak ice box. Magazines — *The New Yorker* and *The Nation* caught her eye — and books — *Gone To Soldiers, Women Who Run With the Wolves,* Blanche Cook's *Eleanor Roosevelt* among them — lay strewn over the tops of end tables as if reluctantly put down. Large, bright prints made the walls interesting.

Danny picked up the most recent *New Yorker* and read movie reviews while Maureen finished a phone conversation. She liked the apartment, and when Maureen placed the receiver in the cradle, she asked about the unusual furniture pieces.

"I bought them up at auction. It's a fun way to collect antiques, cheaper than buying through dealers."

Danny was briefly envious, wishing she had her own place, her own furnishings.

"Would you like a drink before we leave?"

"No, thanks, but please go ahead if you want one."

"No, I'm fine and I'm ready."

"I made reservations at Anthony's. I hope you like Italian food," she said, unlocking the door of the Escort for Maureen and climbing behind the wheel. She cringed at the thought of eating spaghetti in front of this woman, knowing she would never order it, and had to remind herself that Maureen was not some goddess, that she was subject to physical urges and needs just like everyone.

The decor at Anthony's — walls covered with murals of classic Italian scenes, bunches of plastic grapes hanging from lathing tacked to the ceiling and meant to resemble arbors, booths enclosed by fake arches — defined the word *tacky*. But the food here was consistently good.

After being seated in one of the booths, while waiting for drinks, the two women looked at each other. Danny felt suddenly shy, intimidated by Maureen's good looks and amused demeanor. She longed to reach across the table and touch her face.

"So, tell me about yourself," Maureen said, cradling her olive-skinned cheeks in her hands.

"I think you know more about me than I do about you. I was the one interviewed."

"How long have you known Kara?"

"We went to school together, grades K through twelve. Best friends."

"Your resume said you worked and lived in . . . was it Roselawn, Illinois?"

"Yes. I'm in the middle of a divorce." She smiled slightly and lifted her shoulders as if dismissing Roselawn and her marriage.

"Any children?"

"One, a sixteen-year-old girl." Danny stared into space and sighed. "A difficult age, maybe made more so because of circumstances." She returned her gaze to the woman across the table from her.

Maureen nodded as if in sympathetic understanding.

"And you?"

"Never been married, never had children. I moved here from Indiana fifteen years ago. I like Wisconsin."

"What made you move to Edgemont? The job at the Tech?"

A troubled look shadowed the dark eyes. "I almost moved back to Indiana last year. I was offered a job at the Tech in Indianapolis."

Her distress somehow reassured Danny. It lent

Maureen a more human image, implying that she had made mistakes, had suffered lost relationships — just as Michael had intimated.

The waitress set a salad in front of Danny, soup before Maureen and bread in a basket in the middle of the table. The two women ate silently for a few minutes.

"What do you do for fun?" Danny asked, looking up from her chilled salad, wiping her mouth with a napkin.

"Read, listen to music, go to concerts, plays, movies, cook. I like to cook."

Danny wondered what she did to stay in shape, because she definitely had a good body. The silky blouse clinging to pear-shaped breasts attested to that, as did the small firm bottom Danny had admired as it moved in black rayon slacks. "You don't walk or run or ride a bike or swim?" she dared ask.

"I walk, close to an hour a day. I suppose you do more vigorous things." Again the amused smile.

"Mmm," Danny said around a mouthful of bread. "I like to be active," then hastened to add, "but I also like to read and go to concerts and different events." Although Danny had always admired the female jocks, she had never before thought of herself as one of them. Did Maureen look down on physical activity?

The movie should have held Danny's interest, but she found it difficult to focus on anything but the woman next to her. And then, ahead of her a few rows, she saw Tracy's dark head. Acutely conscious of Maureen — of the heady smell of her cologne, of heat whenever their arms or shoulders accidentally touched — Danny was taut with inner tension when the movie ended and the lights went on in the theater.

They stood and Danny led Maureen toward the aisle farthest from Tracy. But in the lobby she came face to face with her daughter and Kim.

Tracy's eyes moved from her mother to Maureen and back again. "Good movie, huh?"

Danny couldn't have said. She introduced the two girls to Maureen, then asked Kim how she was feeling before inquiring, "How'd you two get here?"

"Kim's car."

Danny scowled. She wasn't so distracted by Maureen that she ceased to be a parent. "Are you allowed to drive?" she asked Kim.

"Tracy's driving."

"Be careful and be home on time. Grandma will be there waiting," she cautioned her daughter.

"Terrific," Tracy drawled. "Are you going home now?" Again she looked from her mother to Maureen.

"Not yet," Danny replied in a tone that encouraged no questions.

"She looks like you," Maureen commented as they watched the girls move away toward a group of young people. "What happened to them?"

Danny gave a short laugh. The girls, of course, still carried the scars of their misadventure. "Car accident last weekend. They were both drinking." Monday was Tracy's court date. "Let's go."

They drove in silence to Maureen's apartment. "Why don't you come in for a while?" Maureen asked, causing Danny's heart to hammer erratically.

Nursing a cup of decaffeinated coffee while sitting

on the couch, Danny eyed the books and magazines on the coffee table.

"It was a nice evening. Maybe we can do it again soon," Maureen said quietly from a nearby chair.

"I hope so," Danny replied, but she was so tense she only wanted to flee. Not even Rachel had inspired such emotional strain, and Rachel had been her first woman. She couldn't imagine making love with someone who caused her so much distress. And why? She heard Maureen's voice, saw her head tilt.

"I'm sorry. You said something?"

"Why don't you come to dinner Sunday night? It'll give me a reason to cook and us a chance to talk more."

Was this a signal for her to leave? Danny stood. "Thanks. That'll be nice. What time?"

When she reached home, the nervous tension had drained away, leaving her tired. Shutting the door gently behind her, she walked quietly through the silent house. Upstairs she noticed a light under Charlie's door and tapped lightly.

Charlie, propped up by pillows, looked small in the queen-size bed. "Tracy beat you home. Kara called, said she'd call again tomorrow. Was the movie good?"

"Yeah, it was okay. You'd probably enjoy it. 'Night, Mom." She closed the door softly and moved on down the hall to her own room where she shut herself up with her thoughts.

As the sun pulled up the shade on morning, she awakened from a sex dream. The woman in bed with her, whose hands felt so soft on her skin, vanished with sleep. Running her own hands over her body, she touched the small, firm breasts, the flat abdomen, the slender, strong thighs, and decided that she wasn't such a bad feel. Why should she be so worried about Sunday night? Why had she been so uptight last night?

Kara reached her by phone at the hardware store Saturday morning as Danny put her purse under the counter. "Where were you last night?"

"Out with Maureen."

"That's what I thought." Kara sighed loudly in Danny's ear. "Are you working all day?"

"No, I have this afternoon off."

"Want to go look at the white elephant on Grove Street? I'm showing it to Michael and Tony at three."

"I'd love to."

"Good. I'll pick you up at two or two-thirty. Okay?"

Getting out of Kara's car, Danny gazed in wonder at the immense white house. She walked the brick sidewalk with Kara, Michael and Tony to the open porch which covered the entire front of the house. The interior of the house was empty, cavernous — huge rooms with immense windows and lofty ceilings. Their footsteps, crossing the hardwood and tile floors, echoed off the walls. She admired the handsome woodwork, the wonderful design of the old building.

Once she recovered from the overwhelming size of the dwelling, Danny noticed the neglect. It would require money and work to renovate the building: to paint walls, refinish woodwork, update kitchen facilities, re-carpet, invest in window coverings.

As she wandered through the house, Danny couldn't help but wonder about Michael and Tony's ambitions. Kara followed the two men from room to room, imparting the knowledge she had gleaned about the history of the house and its possible role as a bed and breakfast. Just down the street another house this size had been turned into apartments, reminding Danny of Maureen's place.

"Where will they get a couple hundred thousand dollars?" Danny asked Kara. She had thought the house would cost more. "How can they afford monthly payments?"

"They've got some kind of funding."

It flitted through Danny's mind that a mansion like this would make a fine buddy house, like the one in Roselawn that had housed gay men with AIDS. She had often helped, first with donations, then by offering her time as a volunteer doing whatever needed doing — usually shopping and cooking. She had lost friends in that house, had fought the zoning board along with others to keep the place operating. There had been a lot of furor from the neighbors. She decided against sharing this speculation with Kara, since there was no basis for it.

Kara touched her hand and Danny turned toward her. "How was your date?"

"I have never been so nervous," Danny confessed.

"Did you do it?" Kara stared out the windshield. "Tell me, Danielle," she demanded, after a short silence.

"No. Not this time anyway."

Kara gave her a troubled look. "When are you going to see her again?"

"Sunday. She invited me to dinner. She likes to cook."

More silence followed. "Will you still do it with me when you're doing it with her?" Kara asked.

"Don't ask me that, Kara," Danny pleaded.

Kara reached over and squeezed her hand. "Peter and the kids are gone. Come home with me."

Danny was nervous at first, afraid someone would return home and catch them in the act. She removed Kara's clothes quickly, then shrugged out of her own, thinking they better make this a quickie. But Kara was a wonderful kisser, her lips soft, warm, and responsive, and Danny loved to kiss. When she felt Kara's tongue touch her upper lip, she rolled on top of her and began to move.

Forgetting everything but the present, she buried her face between Kara's breasts, pressing them to her. As she suckled the nipples, she reached inside and felt the moist vaginal walls tighten around her fingers. Drawing out the wetness with each stroke, she spread it over the swelling genitalia.

"Come here," Kara whispered urgently. "Can't we do it together?"

Anchored in an embrace, they coaxed each other to climax.

As the afternoon softened toward evening, fresh air dried and cooled their naked bodies. They lay on the double bed in the guest room at Kara's house. The voices of golfers drifted through the open windows.

Kara had cried out during orgasm but Danny

71

had come quietly and urgently, unable to slow the tide of desire washing over her. She had surged with it, moving with the rhythm of Kara's fingers until her body had broken into spasms, leaving her weak and damp.

They showered together, ate leftovers in the kitchen, and took a long walk before Danny left. Kara, having been uncharacteristically quiet following sex, gave Danny a kiss on the cheek in farewell.

Instead of going home, Danny turned the Escort onto River Road and took it to Lake Drive, which wound along the string of lakes southeast of town. She turned into Pine Lake County Park, drove past tall rows of Norway and white pines, to where the blacktop ended in a small parking lot, and walked to the sandy beach beyond. A Mexican family picnicked nearby, the small dark children screeching as they touched the water with their toes and retreated in haste to the safety of their parents, who lay on a blanket in the sand.

Danny stood for a while at the edge of the lake. Wind blew away the clouds hiding the sun, and she felt its warmth cover her, saw the water turn a sparkling blue, smelled the redolence brought out by the renewed heat. Then she walked the shoreline away from the family at the park. The north side of the lake was undeveloped, its shore rising steeply from a narrow strip of beach. Coming around a bend, she froze at the sight of a doe drinking, water falling from its mouth. Just behind the doe stood a fawn, its ears pricked, its muzzle pressed against its mother's flank. Danny became motionless, but the doe fled with huge bounds up the embankment, pausing at the top for her baby to catch up.

Danny walked on, the ground sandy under her tennis shoes. She wondered where the multitudes of frogs had gone. There had been so many of them, a virtual throng leaping and chunking, when she had come to this lake in her youth.

She had always loved Pine Lake, longing for a place on this north shore where the sun would invariably shine and the summer breezes blow. She had grown up swimming in its waters and the other lakes that were linked together like beads on a chain. She'd picnicked along their banks, necking at night on their beaches, and walked their shores.

As gray clouds took on shades of red from the setting sun, the lake became a mirror for the sky, and she reluctantly turned back toward the county park. The sun slowly sank, taking with it the colors of the day, leaving behind the stars and a half moon to light her way. A whippoorwill called repeatedly from somewhere nearby, and a couple of barred owls carried on a conversation from the woods. Danny stepped up her pace.

The family had left, she noted as she started her engine and drove toward home. Tipsy met her at the door and she bent and stroked his small body, then entered the dining room to find Charlie and Tracy involved in a card game. It was a pleasant surprise to hear their banter.

The game stopped as Tracy eyed her mother expectantly. "Grandma said I had to wait for your okay to go out tonight."

"Where would you go?" Danny asked, sitting at the table with them.

"To Kim's."

"Why don't you have Kim come over here for a change?"

"I guess it's better than doing nothing," Tracy said grudgingly. "You want to finish the game for me, Mom?" she asked, abandoning her cards.

"Sure. Why not?" Danny said obligingly.

That night, as she lay in bed listening to faint conversation and music coming from Tracy's room, she tried again to make sense out of the sexual turn her relationship with Kara had taken. She loved Kara, would never be willing to relinquish their friendship. But she couldn't foresee living with Kara—the children wouldn't cooperate nor did she think Kara would give up her life with Peter.

Maureen? What would it be like if she and Tracy lived with Maureen? She envisioned Tracy's reaction to Danny's sexuality. The image both amused and disturbed her, causing her to smile and squirm. Anyway, how could she possibly share living quarters with someone who unsettled her so? She wouldn't be able to perform the ordinary physical functions of everyday living in the same house with Maureen.

Finally, when the sounds from Tracy's room faded to silence, Danny fell asleep.

VI

Charlie and Danny looked up from their respective sections of the Sunday newspaper when Tracy and Kim straggled into the kitchen. The sun poured through the window above the sink over their young faces, turning them even rosier than sleep had. Tracy stretched and yawned, her legs looking impossibly long and slender under the short nightshirt.

"Let's go to Pine Lake today," Danny suggested. "Have a picnic or something." It wasn't an impulsive idea; she had been wondering how to enjoy the day.

"Oh, Mom." Tracy spoke the words as an exasperated sigh.

"Why not? Look outside. It's gorgeous." It was one of those perfect spring days that tease by offering a taste of summer.

"I think it's a great idea," Kim remarked.

"How about you, Mom?" Danny turned to Charlie, who looked so pleased that Danny experienced a fleeting twinge of guilt and briefly wondered if Charlie often felt left out, unwanted and unsure of her welcome.

Tracy gave Kim a surprised look. "You want to go?"

"Sure. My family hardly ever goes anywhere together. Everyone does their own thing. You know? And Pine Lake's nice."

"What is there to pack for a picnic?" Charlie said more to herself than anyone else. She got up to rummage around in the refrigerator and emerged with her hands full.

It would be a pleasant way to get through this day before going to Maureen's in the evening, Danny mused as she put on shorts and a T-shirt. She galloped down the stairs, followed by Tipsy who somehow knew something exciting was planned and didn't want to be left behind.

"Ma, I'll do this. You go get ready." Danny took over the chore of making sandwiches. Glancing out the window at the sun reaching toward its high point of the day, she felt an urgent need to be outside.

She had feared the county park at Pine Lake would be crowded, but there were only two other young people and a family of four on the beach.

"I feel stupid," Tracy muttered, looking at the boy and girl entwined on a blanket.

"Hey, this is okay," Kim said with a grin.

"What?" Tracy shot back. "Being here with my mother and grandmother? You gotta be kidding."

"Being here with anybody," Kim replied, still smiling.

"I guess," Tracy said with a shrug.

Danny was grateful for Kim's easy acceptance of herself and Charlie. "Anyone want to go for a walk?" she asked.

"I do," Kim said.

Tracy moaned and rolled her eyes but followed them along the same shoreline Danny had walked the evening before.

The dog raced ahead, pausing occasionally to make sure his people were following, sometimes waiting for someone to catch up.

Danny talked to her mother as she walked, telling her of her wish to own some land on the north side of Pine Lake, asking who owned this side of the lake.

"It's easy to find out. I'll pick up a plat book from the courthouse." Charlie kept her gaze on the sand, laced with rocks and weeds and sticks, under her feet. "We used to have some good times out here. Remember? You and your dad and me and Buddy."

"When was the last time you heard from Buddy, Mom?"

Charlie leaped to her son's defense as she always did. "Christmas. He sent a gift. He called."

"How long has it been since you saw him?"

Charlie wrinkled her forehead in thought. "A

couple years ago. Sons marry and they don't need their mother anymore. Such a long ways away." Buddy lived in California. "He wanted me to visit. Maybe I will now that you're back. I didn't want to put Tipsy in a kennel."

Danny suspected that her brother's wife encouraged the lack of communication between mother and son. She remembered the woman as haughty. Perhaps it was the only way he could keep peace between them, but she thought less of her brother for not caring enough to maintain closer contact with his mother. She reached behind her to grasp Charlie's arm. "You all right, Mom?"

Charlie shook her off. "I'm fine. I'm not some old lady yet."

Danny paused at the end of a small peninsula jutting into the lake. It sheltered a cove of water which had always harbored turtles, frogs and shorebirds. A great blue heron flapped into the sky, its long legs trailing. Danny sat on a log in the warm sun and removed her tennis shoes.

With a grunt Charlie lowered herself onto a nearby rock, and Tipsy threw himself at her feet. "The sun feels good, doesn't it?"

Danny spotted the two girls dawdling along the shore, carrying their shoes and wading. She saw them gesturing, heard their voices faint on the soft breeze, and a warm feeling of contentment settled over her.

When Danny arrived at Maureen's, she was still flushed with serenity at the way the day had developed, the rare camaraderie between generations. They had all been reluctant to leave the lake and would have stayed longer had Danny not had this prior commitment. "We'll do this again soon. Okay?" she had suggested as they piled into the Escort for the drive back to Elm Street.

Now she stood hesitantly on Maureen's doorstep, almost wishing she were watching the sun set over Pine Lake instead of catching glimpses of pink and red clouds and sky between buildings and trees. Pushing the doorbell, she heard it ring somewhere inside and waited.

The door opened and Maureen smiled in welcome. She wore what looked like a harem outfit — baggy pants with elastic at the ankles, a sleeveless top, neck high in the front and cut to a low V in the back. The top was a hot pink, the bottom the same color laced with black. Danny smiled her appreciation.

"You took some sun today."

The low, rich tones beckoned Danny inside and again she noticed the peculiar phrasing of Maureen's words. "Yes, I was outside all afternoon." She stood uncertainly in the entryway.

"It looks good on you."

"Thanks." She wanted to add that Maureen looked good just the way she was, pale as a pearl, but she thought the comment inappropriate, considering their uninvolvement.

"Come on in. Join me in a drink."

The ordinary request sounded exotic. Maureen could have asked her if she wanted to use the bathroom and she would probably have enthralled. She pulled herself together to resist this allure. She could drown in it, or worse, make a fool of herself. She sat on the first available chair and smiled brightly.

"Come into the kitchen with me. I've got some last-minute fixings to do." The dark eyes danced with life.

I amuse her, Danny thought as she rose to her feet and followed the smooth back into the kitchen. "Where are you from?" Was this how people talked in Indiana?

"Originally?" Maureen turned and Danny nearly walked into her.

"Yes. Sometimes you say things that no one around here would say. Or shouldn't I ask?"

"I don't mind. You're not the first person to ask that question. My family is from western Pennsylvania. I grew up in the hills." Her rosy lips turned upward at the corners in an irresistible smile. "Now, what would you like to drink?"

"I don't care," Danny answered, smiling like an idiot. "What are you drinking?"

"A white wine."

"That sounds good." She thought it better to drink lightly in order to keep a tight rein on herself. It would be too easy to babble her infatuation. "May I help?"

"Sure. You can set the table."

The dropleaf, oak table, in a nook of the living room, held two placemats, two candles. It appeared cozy, a place to get serious about matters.

When they sat to eat, Maureen lifted her wine glass in a toast. "I'm looking forward to seeing you around the Tech."

"So am I." She did look forward to seeing Maureen in the fall, but she just hated to leave the hardware store. She liked having a job that required no homework, yet wasn't boring.

The menu was Chinese. They began with hot and sour soup, followed by crabmeat Rangoons. The main entree was chicken with broccoli. Danny knew she would have to stretch her imagination to top this dinner with one of her own. She forced herself to eat slowly and sip her wine.

She talked about the store, telling Maureen how much she enjoyed working there and why. In turn Maureen discussed her job and the people who taught at the Tech. The meal seemed quickly over. For dessert Maureen brought out fortune cookies.

"You made these too?" Danny asked, relieved when Maureen shook her head. She read her fortune out loud, "A stranger will come into your life." She smiled. "Maybe that's you. What does yours say?"

Maureen read, "You will inherit a lot of money!" Then added with a short laugh, "That'll be the day."

After dinner they sat on the davenport, one at each end. By this time, instead of being relaxed by the wine, Danny felt strung taut as a piano wire. If Maureen touched her, she thought she might twang; but if she didn't, Danny felt she would burst with the expectation of it. She had considered making the first move herself and decided against it, afraid she might bungle it.

"Do I make you nervous?" Maureen asked with a faint smile.

Feeling herself redden, Danny looked away. Then, suddenly angry for behaving like a teenager, she faced Maureen and found that Maureen had closed some of the distance between them. "Somewhat, yes." The words nearly stuck in her throat and came out sounding strained and thin.

"You make me nervous too." The smile broadened, causing Danny to doubt the words.

She snorted in disbelief. "I can't believe how I feel around you," she blurted and turned away again when she realized what she had said. She felt Maureen's hip touch her own and she sucked air in sudden panic.

"How do I make you feel?" Maureen purred in Danny's ear.

"Like I'm fifteen." She looked into Maureen's eyes, now at a distance of inches. "You look like you find me amusing. Do you?"

Maureen's arm closed over Danny's shoulders. "You're very attractive."

"You're more attractive." Her heart hammered against her chest, pounded in her throat. Danny swallowed to clear the ringing in her ears.

"Do you mind if I kiss you?"

"Do I act like I mind?" She watched Maureen's face close in on her own and shut her eyes as the dark eyes converged. She felt soft, warm lips on hers, a touch of tongue, and she responded with hesitant, gentle kisses and tentative tongue thrusts that quickly became demanding.

When Maureen touched her breast, thumbing her nipple erect, Danny inhaled sharply. It was the anticipation that caused her muscles to tense, waiting for the next move. Her breath caught in her throat as Maureen opened her blouse and reached inside her undershirt.

She cupped Maureen's small, firm breasts —

82

barely a handful apiece. Fumbling with the cloth buttons fastening the harem outfit, she felt Maureen's hand move on down her body and unzip her pants. Freeing her mouth, hardly recognizing her own voice, Danny said, "Can we finish this lying down?"

Maureen stood, her clothes still intact, and took Danny's hand to lead her to the bedroom. Forced to hold her slacks up with her free hand, her blouse open and pulled out of the waistband, Danny felt at a distinct disadvantage. The bedroom was dimly lit by streetlighting creeping around the edges of the blinds.

Danny knew her own body was nice, that it compensated for what it lacked in fullness by being firm and trim and smooth. But she thought Maureen to be perfectly proportioned, feminine, smooth, elegant. After Maureen placed Danny's clothes in a neat pile on a chair, Danny removed the harem outfit and lowered the smaller woman to the bed.

Face to face, they caressed each other. Danny took Maureen's breasts to taste. She wanted to roll her over, to look at the lovely curve of back to hips. But this being their first lovemaking, she refrained. She contained her desire, working her hand between Maureen's legs, surprised that someone so small should feel much the same inside as other women.

When Maureen touched her intimately, Danny gasped. She had been rigid with expectation. As they moved together toward climax, it occurred to Danny that making love with a woman was like making love to oneself; sometimes it was hard to tell the difference between herself and Maureen. Were they experiencing the same sensations, the same exquisite ache? They breathed into each other, their mouths together as if offering the sustenance of life.

Afterward, they lay without talking, fingers inside each other, muscles relaxing, the blood reversing its flow like the tide.

It seemed hardly possible to be standing in court the next day, still in a daze from the previous night's lovemaking. Danny hadn't returned home until four a.m., having fallen asleep in Maureen's bed. She had awakened when Maureen, sighing in sleep, curled against her. Appalled at the passage of time revealed by the bedstand clock, Danny had dressed quietly and kissed a murmuring Maureen goodbye before tiptoeing out into the pre-dawn hush.

"Where were you last night, Mom?" Tracy whispered in her ear.

"Out with a friend," she hissed back, "and we're not here to discuss me."

Charlie was on a bench seat behind them, outside the divider separating the public from the accused and accusing. Kim sat nearby with her mother in attendance. Both girls looked ashen.

Officer Forgarty testified. The judge asked Kim if she admitted to drinking, then administered a long lecture on the illegality and perils of underage drinking, the folly and thoughtlessness and dangers of driving under the influence — although Tracy had not been driving. Tracy hung her head, and Danny felt criminally responsible for her daughter's actions.

The lingering afterglow from the previous night,

which had favorably affected all her relationships this day, vanished with the sternness of the judge's voice and the seriousness of his words. Danny now felt like a bad mother, negligent in her duties, unable to control her daughter.

"Can we wait for Kim to be done?" Tracy asked in the hallway after being ordered to attend a course on drug and alcohol abuse.

"No." Danny spoke quickly, still angered for having been made to feel so guilty. "I have to get back to the hardware store and you have to go to school."

"He sure had a lot of unkind things to say, didn't he?" Charlie commented as the three of them walked out of the building. "How are parents supposed to watch their kids twenty-four hours a day?"

Mildly surprised, Danny glanced at Charlie. "I don't know, Ma. You want to drop Tracy off at school?"

Charlie nodded, and Danny stood on the courthouse steps watching them walk to the Buick: the long-legged girl in jeans and a cotton, short-sleeved sweater, the older woman in polyester pantsuit and short-cropped, gray hair. Danny felt a smile forming. Charlie refused to give up her polyester outfits, insisting they would come back in style, even as Tracy pretended despair at such poor fashion taste. She could hear their voices, the old teenage lament followed by refusal.

"Let me drive, Grandma," Tracy begged.

"I'll drive, tootsie. Don't you ever know when you're in the doghouse?"

"Grandma, you drive about two miles an hour."

And never use your turn signals and stop at all the corners even when there's no stop sign, Danny added silently before hurrying to the Escort. The weather, threatening rain, had turned cold as it often did in May.

She felt as if she had been away from work for more than a day and a half. So much had happened in that short time. She put her purse under the counter and donned the employee's smock with her name sewn over the left breast pocket. Her body tingled as if Maureen's hands were still on her.

"Hi. Remember me?"

Danny turned and recognized Chris Bauman, wearing a smock like her own. "You're going to work here?"

"I can't find a full-time position teaching phys ed. I've been substituting all winter. So, I decided to give this a try." She looked tan and relaxed and pleased with herself.

"Well, good. I like working here. I hope you do too."

When Danny parked next to the Regal that afternoon, she felt less tired than she had after leaving court that morning. Training Chris had not only sped the workday, but made it fun.

With his tail wagging his entire body, Tipsy met her at the door. Tantalizing odors from the oven filled her nostrils. "Smells good, Mom," she called.

She found Charlie reading the paper in the living room. A light turned on against the overcast, cool day, made the room look dismal on this spring afternoon.

"I got the plat book." Charlie shoved the orange, plastic-bound paperback toward her. "Let me warn you, though. There's one strange man who owns most of the land on that side of the lake. You ever heard of him, Raymond Dupris?"

Danny shook her head. "You know him?"

"Never laid eyes on the man. They were talking about him in the courthouse."

"How is he strange?"

"He lives alone with his dogs in a shack on the land. Someone said he had no electricity or running water. He hunts out of season. Traps, runs coons with the dogs. Wants nothing to do with people."

When she had her share of the proceeds from the sale of the house she and Craig owned, she planned to make an offer on some of this man's land. She took the plat book and paged through it to the township where Pine Lake lay, shaped like a boomerang. Absently, she remarked, "That means he's got no phone either."

"Probably not. That would be a nice piece of land to own. Eighty-five acres there. It's worth a lot of money."

"I expect he knows that too. I'd just want a slice with maybe a hundred feet or more of lake frontage." She looked up from the map to see Charlie's eyes narrowed, her lips pursed, forehead creased. Danny sighed and silently begged her mother not to say what she thought she was thinking.

"I wouldn't mind having a lot on the lake either.

Maybe I could sell this house and buy a piece of property, build a smaller place on it. At my age you can sell without paying capital gains."

"Mom, I need my own place."

"So do I, sweetie, so do I."

"You want to be my neighbor?"

"Not so close that you could tell me what to do all the time."

Danny couldn't believe her ears. She thought the opposite was closer to the truth and said so.

"Danny, I love you. You know that. But you're always trying to bend my will to yours."

Could that be so? Danny must have looked as dumbfounded as she felt. Was she so controlling? "No, Mom."

"Yes, Danny. We all do it. I want to do things my way, you think your way is best, Tracy wants things her way. It's a constant battle. Remember the thermostat war, the telephone skirmishes, the television battles?"

Danny interrupted. "I don't even like to watch TV."

"That's just it. I do." Charlie placed a cool, dry hand over Danny's.

The skin felt paper thin. Mulling over her mother's words, Danny rubbed it gently between her fingers. "Well, I agree we need our own homes."

"We don't have to be miles apart. We'll see plenty of each other."

And here she had worried about telling her mother that she needed her own space. Danny smiled a little. "I thought you were going to suggest we buy and build together."

"I know you did." Charlie freed her hand enough to pat her daughter's.

The back door opened and closed. They heard Tracy talking to the dog. "Smell that good food. I'm famished. Where is everyone?"

In his exuberance Tipsy let out a joyous bark of welcome.

VII

May turned into June. Danny spent weekend nights in Maureen's bed. The anticipation of it and the act itself thrilled her as much as the first time had, but she was no more at ease. Every time she thought her heart might pound its way out of her chest. And she still felt like a guest at royalty's table, perhaps even the jester.

She took up tennis with Chris, playing on the courts in the park near Elm Street where the river flowed past. They often drove there after leaving the hardware store and spent long, warm evenings pursuing a tennis ball.

Danny played to work off a restlessness which only activity satisfied. Chris's seemingly endless energy brought out the competitor in Danny. Oftentimes, Kara watched from a park bench, cheering whoever managed to lob the ball across the net.

Afterwards, they would sit near the water and watch it rush by. If the sunset turned spectacular, they lingered until the best color faded from sky and river before making their respective ways home.

Kara informed them one evening, when the western horizon looked as if it were smeared with bright finger-paints, that Michael and Tony had bought the large house on Grove Street. "They didn't buy it alone. Some organization provided them with some funding."

"What organization?" Danny asked, her gaze glued to the sky. Soft breezes dried the sweat she had worked up during the matches, and her leg and arm muscles tingled pleasantly.

"I can't remember. Some acronym."

Chris glanced up. "Are they going to need help renovating?"

"I would think so. It needs a face-lift, doesn't it, Danny?"

Danny looked at her friend and felt desire move. Kara looked wonderful — her cheeks rosy, her blue eyes alive, her skin tan and glowing. Her breasts were barely concealed by a T-shirt. She could almost feel their considerable weight in her hands. When her eyes rose to meet Kara's, she saw the crooked grin of acknowledgment, the slightly elevated eyebrows, as if to ask when. She cleared her throat. "Certainly does."

Had Chris caught this unspoken exchange? As if they both had the same thought, they turned their attention to Chris. But Chris, arms wrapped around sun-browned legs, stared at the river and sky. She seemed unaware of the passion in the air. "I think I'll ask them if they need help," she said.

Danny studied Chris's hair, curling down the back of her head and neck, the tips bleached by sunlight. "I was thinking of doing that myself."

"Well, let's make it a threesome. We could offer our services right now. They might be there. Closing was this afternoon." Kara stood and straightened her shorts.

Michael met them by the front porch where he was examining the overgrown shrubbery. His long skinny body was clothed in a flimsy tank top and shorts. Red, curly hair sprouted around the top of the shirt with its message, *Life Is A Beach*. His gangling legs and arms were burned a bright red through the covering of thick, reddish hair. "What do you think, girls? A clip here and there?"

"A clip everywhere. Junipers grown out of control," was Kara's response.

"Sure, now you tell us our shrubbery sucks — after we buy the place." He straightened and grinned at them. "Come to visit? The tea's not even here yet, not to mention the liquor."

"Let me handle the bushes," Kara said. "Trust me. I'll make your lawn the envy of the neighbors."

It was funny, Danny thought, how you noticed

things you missed the first time — like the neighborhood, which once must have been elegant, now gone a little seedy.

"Good. We're going to need all the help we can get."

"And we're here to offer it," Chris said.

Michael smiled wryly. "You have no idea what you're offering."

Danny disputed that. "Yes, I think Kara and I do, anyway. I don't know if Chris has seen the house."

"Well, come on in then." Michael herded them onto the porch and into the house.

Only Kara held back. "I've got to go home. Put me in charge of lawn and garden."

"Wait." Danny followed her onto the front sidewalk. "Want to go to dinner tomorrow night and catch up on things?" Dinner together was usually eaten in bed somewhere.

Kara grinned and winked. "Sure. I'll call you at work tomorrow."

After Michael ushered Chris through the house, he stood with her and Danny on the front porch under a yellow light effectively dimmed by a covering of dead and live bugs. "We're going to start with the bedrooms on Saturday. You don't have to help, you know. It's wonderful that you want to, and of course we'd never turn you down."

Danny committed herself. "I'll be here. It'll be fun."

"Me too," Chris promised.

The two women had driven over in Danny's Escort, leaving Chris's car at the park. "Nice of you to offer to help." Danny glanced at Chris in the darkened car and was rewarded with a smile.

"Nice of you, too," Chris replied, her fingers grazing Danny's knee.

Startled, Danny stiffened and almost involuntarily jerked her leg away from the unexpected touch. Hoping that Chris had meant nothing by it, she wondered if she should just pretend she hadn't noticed. But then she felt Chris's nails gently rake her leg from knee to upper thigh. Her skin tingled tantalizingly in their wake.

Now what? Was she supposed to continue conversing as if nothing was going on? Was there such a shortage of available lesbians in town that she was in constant demand? Maureen on the weekends; Kara during the week. When would she squeeze in Chris? During lunch? She smiled fleetingly at the thought. All-too-familiar desire stirred within her, but she placed her hand over Chris's, stopping its progress. "I can't."

"Why not? We like the same things. It could be great fun."

"You mean we could play tennis and racquetball and ski and hike and camp together?"

"Yes. I think we're very compatible." Chris's voice had a sweet, pleading melody to it.

Danny steeled herself against it. "We can do those things now." She turned the last corner to the park and stopped behind Chris's Toyota. With the engine still running, Danny turned to Chris. "Look, if I wasn't involved already, I certainly would be interested."

"I don't give up easily." Chris extricated herself

from the car and bent over to talk through the open door. "Thanks for the lift. I'll see you tomorrow."

Danny watched her walk to her car and waited for it to start before she headed for home.

She found Tracy and Kim in the kitchen, popping popcorn. Ever since the outing at Pine Lake, Kim had spent many days and nights at their house. It was a relief to Danny not to have to worry about Tracy's whereabouts.

"This is the second night this week you missed dinner, Mom." Tracy stood with arms crossed.

"I was playing tennis. You should come and watch sometime. You could even play. The courts are right down the street."

Tracy, who had never exhibited any interest in sports, looked indifferent.

"We should do that," Kim said.

Tracy rolled her eyes. "Sure, Kim. That's right up on top of the list of exciting things to do."

Danny asked, "How's the drug and alcohol class going?" She sensed a studied casualness following the question.

Tracy shrugged as if bored. "Lots of gory movies and lectures and stuff like that. People coming in to tell us horror stories."

Kim continued, "This one kid told us he killed a whole family while driving under the influence, that he has to live with that. He tried to kill himself at first but now he goes around lecturing to groups like us and in high schools. It was pretty awful."

"Do you think hearing those things keeps anyone from drinking and driving?"

The girls nodded vigorously, but Danny remained

unconvinced. Fear of getting caught again would probably be more effective. Kids too often thought unthinkable things only happened to other people. "Where's Grandma?"

"Reading the paper. She left some food in the oven for you."

She was starved, but she didn't expect Charlie to cook for her every day and then keep it warm when she was late. Drawn to the oven by hunger, she filled a bun with sloppy joes, spooned German potato salad onto a plate and went into the living room to sit with Charlie while she ate.

Charlie wore a new look, a frizzy perm which at first she had professed to hate. When she came home from the Mane Tamers with her hair tightly curled and her eyelids shaded beige, she went upstairs to the bathroom and attempted to comb the curls straight. Danny complimented her in vain. But when Tracy walked in the door and said, "Wow, Grandma, you look great," Charlie had apparently accepted her granddaughter's judgment.

Lately, Danny caught Charlie sneaking smiling looks in every mirror she passed. Sometimes her eyelids were beige, sometimes blue or gray or green, but never bare of shadow. She had even taken to painting her fingernails.

The next day, during a lull at the check-out counters, Kara called while Danny and Chris were talking. "I'll meet you at the usual place. Okay? Five-thirty or shortly after?"

The usual place was the Budget Inn about seven miles out of town. "Sure. Should I pick up some deli?"

"Sounds good. Got to go now. Another deal in the works."

"You must have made a bundle off the place on Grove Street."

"I did, but it was a long dry spell before that. It all comes out in the wash. See you later. Looking forward."

Did Kara always talk in phrases? Danny couldn't recall. She looked forward too, she realized. Having forgotten Chris's presence, she noticed her interest and flushed a little.

"Kara?"

"Yes," Danny replied cautiously.

"Is she the competition?"

"She's my best friend, Chris. Let it go. Okay?" She couldn't handle any more than two women, anyway, Danny thought. Kara's marriage made this juggling act possible. She could counter Kara's protests about her sleeping with Maureen by pointing out Kara's marital status. And she thought that Maureen was unaware of her affair with Kara. If Maureen suspected there was someone else, she never said anything about it.

Parking several cars down from Kara's Grand Am, she walked to the office. She usually was the upfront person, who signed for the room. Kara was too afraid someone would recognize her.

"You're not married," Kara had pointed out. "It's okay for you to fool around."

The clerk, a huge woman and someone new, eyed her with interest. "Room two-forty-two, honey. You look familiar."

It was silly of her to assume that these people at

97

the motel never saw her around town. "Do I?" Nosy woman, she thought and took the key without making eye contact.

"Have a nice day."

"Thanks," she mumbled as she went out the door into the June heat. It was a little hot for so early in the season, but it felt good to Danny. She liked to sweat in the summer—the hotter the better.

She knocked on Kara's closed window and continued walking. She heard a car door slam and Kara's footsteps on the sidewalk. Without turning, she said, "You shouldn't run your car when it's parked, just so you can have the air on."

"You want me all sweaty?" Kara asked, catching up.

"I like you sweaty."

"I like you any way." Kara slid an arm through Danny's.

Unlocking the door to the room, Danny shut it behind them. She tossed her purse next to Kara's on the dresser and looked at the two of them in the mirror. They smiled at their reflection.

Thinking about Chris's surprising interest in her, Danny asked, "Do you find me very attractive, Kara?"

"I think you're a knockout." Kara ran her hands up Danny's bare arms. "You're all different shades of brown. Your skin is tan, your eyes that smoky hazel, your hair auburn."

"I sound like mud," Danny muttered.

"So, do you find me attractive?" Kara asked.

Slowly, Danny nodded. "I always have. You're sort of luscious. Beautiful eyes, beautiful skin, wonderful breasts, and you always smell good."

Kara laughed. "Interesting what you find attractive. I love your body. It's so tight and you move with such control, such grace."

"And I like yours." She meant it too, she thought as she pulled Kara close. Maureen was elegant, Kara exuberant. Chris probably stood somewhere in between. Briefly, she considered telling Kara about Chris's advances and then put away the idea; Kara got upset enough about Maureen.

Making love with Kara had its own distinct flavor. Their inhibitions dropped from them at every opportunity. They had found themselves wrapped around each other on the floor, or on someone's couch, or standing, or in a car on a dark night — as surprised by their passion as a stranger might be.

With Maureen she carefully guarded her feelings — never unleashing that ardor, never really letting down her hair, so to speak. Still, making love with Maureen literally took her breath away. She treated it as a fragile, precious act to be treasured, something she enjoyed perhaps more when reliving it in her mind.

Hastily, they removed their clothes and fell on the bed in close embrace. Kara's fullness comforted Danny — the feel of skin on skin, breasts on breasts, legs entangled. She breathed a sigh of pure pleasure into Kara's mouth as she caressed her satiny skin.

Slowly seeking each other with their mouths and hands, they made prolonged love—hanging on the brink of climax as long as possible. Danny had never enjoyed sex as much with anyone as she now did with Kara. Never had it been so relaxed, so much fun.

Afterward, while eating submarine sandwiches

and potato chips in bed, Kara said, "I want to leave Peter, Danny."

"What?" For some reason, perhaps because she wasn't prepared and didn't want to hear this now, Danny was astounded. "Why?"

Kara's blue eyes pleaded. "I can't stay with Peter and continue to do this with you."

Danny crossed her arms, steeling herself against Kara's wishes. "We can't live together, you know. Peter or the kids might suspect."

"Why couldn't we? We've been best friends forever. Who else would I turn to? We could easily afford an apartment together."

"I don't want to be responsible for this."

"You're not, Danny. I told you a long time ago I had thoughts of leaving Peter."

"I don't want a relationship, Kara, and that's what it would be now that we're sexual."

Kara looked hurt. She crossed her arms. "I didn't suggest a relationship. And how do you know you don't want to live with me when we haven't even tried it?"

Danny relented a little. "Don't leave him now. This is all new to you. Maybe it isn't what you want. Give yourself some time, Kara."

Before showering together they made love again, then left for their separate homes.

Saturday Danny and Kara arrived at the house on Grove Street together. The hot weather still held them captive. They escaped it with air conditioning, though Danny hated being forced indoors by the heat. She and Chris had called off Friday's tennis match. Surrounded by trees, with large windows open and high ceiling fans whirring, the house felt cool when they walked through the empty rooms.

There were guys there, not just Michael and Tony, Kevin and Mark, but others she had never met who must have come with the unfamiliar cars parked in the driveway — some with out-of-state license plates.

Chris was among them and greeted Danny and Kara with a question. "Sleep in, you two?"

It was nine o'clock and already eighty-five degrees. Danny had slept poorly because of the heat. "How did you get out of working this morning?"

"Told him I couldn't come in today."

"Hmm. I'm surprised Brad didn't call me."

"He probably did after you left the house."

Michael put Kara and Danny to work stripping off wallpaper in an empty bedroom, where Chris joined them. Kara said the shrubbery could wait for a cooler day.

"Where did all these guys come from?" Danny asked, when the three of them were alone.

"Friends, I guess."

"Do you know what he and Tony are doing here?" Kara asked.

"What?" Danny asked, sure that Kara was going to confirm her suspicions — that this place was going to offer shelter to people with AIDS.

"They're going to turn this building into not only a bed and breakfast, but a hospice for those with AIDS. You can spend your vacation here, helping the less fortunate — financially and otherwise. It's an interesting concept."

"But if you have AIDS, you don't have to pay?"

"Only what you can afford. That's my understanding anyway."

Even though the information came as no surprise, Danny felt touched by annoyance. "Well, why the hell didn't you say so before now?"

"Michael and Tony asked me not to until after closing."

"You couldn't even tell *me*?" Danny asked, aggrieved.

Kara shrugged and brushed damp hair out of her eyes. "I am telling you."

Chris said, "But they're not doing anything illegal — not by renting rooms. Are they? This area looks like it's going to apartments."

Danny remarked, "I wouldn't think so as long as it's not construed as some kind of nursing home."

A radio in a nearby room sent the sounds of Eric Clapton singing "Tears in Heaven" through the third floor. Kara ended the discussion. "Well, ladies, let's get to work. I don't want to do this all summer."

Halfway through the day, Michael brought Maureen to the room where the three women were now washing wallpaper paste off the stripped walls. Maureen wore khaki shorts and a cream-colored blouse. Along with Chris and Kara, Danny was covered with dirty little pieces of wallpaper, her hair disheveled, her clothes glued to her with sweat. Maureen looked like an ad from a fashion magazine.

Danny wiped her face with a forearm and tried to stand. Her back felt broken from sliding herself across the floorboards, wiping off the baseboards. "You're going to help, too?"

"I'm going to run errands for Michael and Tony."

Disappointed, but thinking it appropriate that Maureen was given an easy job, Danny was just glad to see her. She wanted to follow the trim figure out of the room and tell her how much she looked forward to dinner that night at her apartment. She wiped her hands on her shorts and stood up with a grunt.

"You okay?" Kara asked, watching Danny straighten.

Danny spoke a little curtly. "I'm fine. Hurts to stand up after sitting like that for a while."

Kara pointed out, "Don't I know it. I've been bending over for hours."

Danny went through the door after Maureen, who turned and said solicitously, "We can make dinner a little later if you like."

"Seven's fine. You look marvelous."

Maureen picked wallpaper out of Danny's hair and gave her that amused smile. "So do you."

That evening Maureen opened the door dressed in cotton shorts and halter top. Eyeing appreciatively the swell of hips swinging below the nearly bare back, Danny followed her to the kitchen.

"I moved North partly to escape from suffocating heat."

"I like it," Danny said, leaning against the counter. "Summer was made for sweating."

Maureen shot her an incomprehensible look. "Pigs are made for sweating."

"Actually, pigs don't sweat," Danny replied. "That's why they wallow in the mud, to cool off. Someday I'll live on a lake. Then when it's hot, I'll make like a pig."

"Sounds idyllic," Maureen said dryly. She stood with one hand on the refrigerator door and eyed Danny. "Would you like a gin and tonic?"

"Sure. Do you enjoy the water?"

"I never learned to swim."

"I'd like to take you to my favorite lake. I'll teach you to swim."

Maureen took gin out of the freezer and tonic from the refrigerator door. "Why don't you do the honors? You make such good drinks."

"We could go to Pine Lake tomorrow."

"I prefer swimming pools where I know what's on the bottom and where it is."

Danny poured the gin over ice, added tonic, a slice of lemon, an olive and a little olive juice, and stirred the concoction. "You don't have to get in the water, you know."

"Then why go?"

Why indeed? Danny asked herself. She could go with Tracy or Charlie or maybe Kara. Or she could work at the house on Grove Street. She dropped the subject, but there remained an empty space where hope for a mutual interest had been slotted.

When they finally went to bed, Danny felt exhausted from the day's work and anticipation of this moment. No matter how she prepared herself mentally to be with Maureen, the woman had a strange effect on her. She turned wet not only between her legs but between her ears, she concluded with disgust.

Now they lay together, having temporarily satisfied that unquenchable fire burning in Danny. She didn't know whether the same desire flared in Maureen; she doubted it. But she couldn't seem to control or quell the longing Maureen unleashed in her.

"Would you like to be in a relationship?" she murmured into Maureen's slender neck.

"You mean move in together?"

"Yes." Danny rose on one elbow and looked into the dark eyes, suddenly gone opaque.

Maureen's voice became curiously flat. "I don't think so. I did that once. It didn't work."

"That was with someone else," Danny argued, but she felt more relief than anything else at the refusal.

Maureen, her eyes so black and without luster as to resemble two pieces of burnt charcoal, swung her legs over the side of the bed and stood up in an uncharacteristically quick movement. "I like living alone."

"Okay. We won't talk about it then," Danny said quickly. What could possibly have happened to set off such an emotional upheaval? Danny could have cut her own tongue out for asking the question. "I'm sorry I brought it up. Now come on back to bed."

Maureen stood like a lovely, ivory statue on the Oriental rug. "Maybe you should go."

"I said I'm sorry. I promise to never say anything more on the subject."

Slowly, Maureen lowered herself to the bed.

"Come here." Folding Maureen in her arms, Danny gently rocked her until she felt her muscles relax, her breathing even out. Was she asleep? She ran a hand over the small back, curving in then out over the swell of bottom. She kissed her forehead, her cheeks and eyelids and chin, her soft mouth. No response. Continuing the gentle caressing, Danny circled her thighs, her abdomen and breasts — all the while watching the finely etched features. Maureen's lids fluttered, her breathing quickened and Danny's fingers slid easily in the triangular tangle of black curls.

VIII

The house on Grove Street became a cause for Danny. She spent many nights there working during the long evening hours — removing wallpaper and washing walls, painting and repainting, sanding down woodwork and staining. She worked with Chris and Kara and sometimes Maureen. Michael and Tony and Kevin and Mark were usually in some other part of the house.

Kara put up wallpaper, meticulous in measuring and cutting, yet able to do a large room in a day. She sang to the tunes on the radio as she worked.

Maureen, when she showed up, usually trimmed with paint or stain. As she dabbed at walls or woodwork, she chewed on her tongue and scowled in concentration. Chris and Danny rolled paint onto ceilings and walls with long strokes, first one direction then the other. As they covered large areas quickly, they bantered with each other and whomever was nearby. Sometimes the conversation took a serious turn, but not for long.

Chris and Danny played tennis before work twice a week, then usually returned to the house on Grove Street in the evening to continue their renovation. It was during one of these evenings that Michael brought Tracy and Kim to Danny, who thought at first he was just coming to sit on the floor and talk, as he often did.

"*Hola,* ladies. You have visitors."

Danny looked down from the board stretched between two ladders and nearly lost her balance. Paint dripped from the roller onto the two-by-eight on which she stood, and she dropped to a sitting position. "Tracy, is something wrong?"

"No. Kim and I were playing tennis and I wanted to see where you went nights."

Danny introduced the two girls, and Michael took Tracy's hand between his and held it a moment. "You've missed your mother, haven't you? She's been a godsend to me."

Chris set down the roller to wipe her hands on her shorts, so that she could shake their hands.

"Want to see the house?" Michael asked. Danny knew he loved showing off the place. Each time, he said, he saw it through someone else's eyes and gained some new perspective. He looked bizarre, she thought, rather like a Raggedy Andy scarecrow.

Tracy hesitated, then said quickly, "Sure. But Mom, I came to tell you I'm going to work at McDonald's starting tomorrow, me and Kim."

"What?" Danny frowned. "You should have talked to me first."

"I'm seventeen, Mom. Everyone works. Even Grandma."

"Since when does Grandma work?"

"She started at the IGA last week. You just haven't been home long enough to find out."

"Why didn't she tell me?"

"I don't know. That's all she talks about, who did what where. She picks it up at the store."

Danny felt like an unobservant lout, so wrapped up in her own doings that she failed to see what those closest to her were up to. She warned, "Once school starts you'll have to quit."

"Maybe." Tracy sidled toward the door where Michael and Kim waited.

"Not maybe, kiddo."

"All the kids at school work."

"You're not all the kids. School is work, your most important job."

Tracy shrugged and fled the room.

Danny wanted to hurry after her daughter and impress the importance of good grades and learning. But talk was usually wasted on Tracy.

"I wondered when I'd meet your daughter," Chris said, grinning.

"And what's so funny?"

"It's just kind of hard to think of you as a mother, especially an irritated one."

"That's funny?"

Chris laughed. "I wondered while I was listening if your mother talked to you the way you talk to your daughter, because mine did."

"You're saying the language of parents doesn't change. That's not a new observation." Danny stood up on the board and dipped her roller into the tray of paint.

"Well, I don't know about that. I don't have any kids." She, too, rolled her roller in paint and covered a section of wall with it.

"Why do you have trouble thinking of me as a mother?"

"Probably because this is the first time I saw you that way. I could get used to it."

"It doesn't take any talent to become a mother. To be a success at the job does, though." She grunted as she rolled the ceiling over her head.

Out of the blue, Chris asked, "It's Maureen, isn't it?"

"I'm not in the mood, Chris," Danny warned. "And you're not going to surprise me into answering."

Chris apparently had meant it when she said she didn't give up easily. She had settled into a low-key pursuit of Danny since that first evening. They spent a lot of time together — playing tennis, working at Morgan Hardware and at Michael and Tony's big old house.

"I know it's Maureen, that you see her on the

weekends. I also know you spend time with Kara during the week."

"So? I'm with you during the week and on the weekends, too." For the life of her, Danny couldn't understand the attraction these women had for her — although she thought she might just be a convenience for Maureen.

Kara, pressing both hands into the small of her back, walked into the room. "I thought I saw Michael shepherding your daughter and her friend around like a couple of princesses."

"Sometimes Tracy acts like she is a princess," Danny said, glancing at Kara. "Are you all right?"

"Just stretching. That bending and cutting and measuring and pasting are hard on the back, especially when you're carrying around a few extra pounds like I am. I'll admit that I'm not as young and limber as I used to be, Danielle. I won't get all huffy about it like you."

"I wasn't huffy."

"You were too. You jump through hoops for you know who, the prima donna." But Kara's tone and smile belied her words.

Danny said defensively, "I wouldn't jump through hoops for God."

Kara's smile grew into a broad grin. "You might if God were a woman."

Michael reappeared soon after with Tracy and Kim in his wake. "I've shown the girls my mansion and they want to help. Got anything for them to do that won't dirty their clothes permanently?"

"I can use some help," Kara said.

At home that evening, Danny knocked on

Charlie's bedroom door. Supported by pillows and with a small bedside lamp lighting the book she read, Charlie looked up over her glasses at her.

"I hear you're working at the IGA."

Charlie nodded. "I got bored and there was a help wanted sign in the window. So, one day I applied, the next they hired me. I wondered how much time would pass before you found out."

"Why didn't you say something?"

"I thought maybe you'd come in the store one day and see me at the check-out counter." Charlie smiled a little.

Danny went to the side of the bed. "Do you like it?"

"It keeps me busy, and it's only part-time. Stop in and see me at work sometime." She reached for Danny's hand and squeezed it.

"I will, Mom. Tipsy is going to be lonely with all of us gone at least part of the day."

The dog lifted his head from his corner basket and wagged his tail.

Danny tingled with excitement. Craig had just told her there had been an acceptable offer on the house. She didn't know how he felt about selling the home they owned together and tried to keep the joy out of her voice. "Can you send the papers for me to sign?"

"Sure. There's no need for you to even attend closing. We can do it by mail." He paused. "How are you, Danny?"

She only talked to him now when they had to

discuss Tracy or had business to settle. "Good. I start working at the Tech here in the fall."

"Tracy told me."

"And you?"

"Okay. I'm not living at home anymore."

"Does Tracy have your address and phone number?"

"I was going to give it to her now."

She handed Tracy the phone and heard her say, "Hi, Dad, how are ya?" before leaving the room. Bounding upstairs to her room with Tipsy on her heels, she wanted to shout her happiness. Finally she'd have enough money to make an offer on some land.

Lying on her double bed, she watched the play of light and wind on the leaves of the ash tree outside the window. Thoughts bounced around her mind like balls in a pinball machine, ricocheting off other thoughts, lighting up ideas and spawning doubts. Before she actually spent anything, she'd have to have in hand the settlement money from Craig. She could, though, approach Dupris.

She rolled onto her side, facing the window, and felt the dog's tongue on her hand. "Poor Tips. You miss Charlie, don't you?" The animal dogged Danny's footsteps when Charlie was gone.

Danny had been at the IGA after work and checked out at her mother's counter. They had talked a few moments before Danny picked up her groceries and left.

Danny felt the bed sag behind her and heard Tracy's accusing voice, "Dad told me our house is sold."

Danny turned onto her back and looked at the

girl. To see her daughter sulky again, after so many weeks of comparative pleasantry, dismayed Danny. She had forgotten how much she disliked Tracy's sullen moods. She said gently, "We have to settle, honey."

The girl announced, "I'm going to visit Dad next week."

"Good," Danny replied. "Are you hungry?"

"Kind of. Are you?"

"I'll fix us something." She stood and stretched. "Aren't you still working at McDonald's?"

Tracy looked at her feet. Her face had that painful, pinched look that made Danny want to hold and shake her at the same time. "School's going to start in a couple weeks. You said I had to quit then."

With a hug and a smile, Danny attempted to convey support and love — all the positive feelings she felt for her daughter. "Come on, sweetie, and help me. We'll make something good and save some for Grandma."

Taking advantage of the delicate situation, or so Danny thought, Tracy asked, "Can I take the car to Dad's, Mom?"

"And what will I drive while you're gone?" When Tracy failed to reply, Danny continued, "We'll get you there, honey, but not in the car."

"Maybe Grandma will let me drive hers. She walks to work."

"Ask her," Danny said, certain that Charlie would refuse.

* * * * *

114

The heat wave had run nonstop all summer, but it had not kept Danny from many of her pursuits. She and Chris only occasionally cancelled tennis. Danny and the others who had started work on Michael and Tony's large house continued until it looked fresh and clean and new inside. With the interior redone, Michael and Tony turned to exterior work, scraping and painting the outer walls. Even as they did so, guests began arriving.

As promised, Kara had turned the yard into a semblance of respectability. With help, she trimmed the shrubbery and planted lilac bushes and yews and creeping juniper, put in beds of bright flowers — impatiens, marigolds, rosebushes, daisies, phlox, poppies — and coaxed them into blooming health, encouraged the growth of thick, green grass with the aid of fertilizer and generous doses of water. She had given up waiting for the heat to pass and sweated under a wide-brimmed hat.

Danny could not help but admire her well-endowed figure with an occasional pat on the rump when Kara bent to her tasks. She was sure the neighbors thought Kara was Michael's wife or at least his girlfriend.

"You would never slap Maureen on the fanny," Kara remarked, swatting Danny's hand away.

Danny realized that was true but refused to admit it. Instead, she looked around the yard admiringly. "You do nice work, Kara."

Kara squinted up at Danny, her blue eyes slits against the glare of sun. "Thanks, darling."

They had talked over the possibility of Kara

115

leaving Peter until they gave up the topic out of boredom, having gone round and round and gotten nowhere. After their last argument along these lines, Kara avoided talking to Danny for a week, which disturbed Danny much more than she thought it would or should. The next week, though, they had put their disagreements to rest in bed at the Budget Inn. Still, lurking just behind every conversation lay the unresolved dispute. Their lovemaking, however, had not suffered — if anything, it had become more passionate.

Danny shifted from foot to foot, her gaze meeting and wavering from the blue slashes.

"You have something to tell me?" Kara asked impatiently, a clump of weeds hanging from one soiled hand.

"I talked to Craig last night. The house is sold. I want to see this Dupris guy about buying a lot on the lake. I wondered if you would go with me."

Kara's eyebrows arched. "You don't want to live with me but you want me to help you get your own place?"

Had she actually said that? She couldn't remember. "Kara, I never said I didn't want to live with you. I just said I wasn't sure I wanted an exclusive relationship. You should know I'd never turn you away, but I don't think you've had enough time to make a decision as drastic as leaving Peter."

"I haven't made that decision yet," Kara snapped. "I had to know what might be in store for me if I did."

Michael, paint scraper in hand, climbed down

from a ladder and meandered in their direction. "Isn't this great? The second week with guests."

Danny put a smile on her face. "I'm glad."

He plunged into the middle of their disagreement. "What is going on with you two? Every time I sneak up on you, which is never intentional, you're arguing about something. I hate to see you fight."

"Sorry." Kara attempted to brush the dirt off her hands and glared at Danny.

"Can I mediate?" he asked.

Danny looked at Kara. "Thanks, Michael, but it's just something we have to work through."

"Speaking of work. I've got to clean up and get at it," Kara said. "I have a showing in a couple hours."

"You know, you two made a big difference here. Tony and I can never thank you enough. We're going to put on a huge dinner the second Saturday after Labor Day for all our friends. Mark your calendars."

"Do you need help?" Danny asked.

"Nope. This one is on us. It's our thanks." Michael walked away but not before saying, "Make up, girls. Whatever it is, it's not worth it."

"Well?" Danny said, eyeing Kara again.

Kara sighed and caved in. "When and where?"

"Where is going to be the problem. We have to find him. I thought maybe after work tomorrow, around five-thirty." She felt her heart climb into her throat.

The next day she picked Kara up at her house. As they drove out of town, Kara reached for Danny's hand. "Where does this guy live?"

"On the north side of Pine Lake."

"I could have strangled you yesterday. You dismiss me as if I'm a child."

Danny's heart sank; she wanted no more futile disagreements. "What you do mean?"

"You said you'd take me in as if doing me a favor, as if an afterthought. And you talk like I haven't given serious consideration to the consequences of leaving Peter. Did I discourage you when you left Craig? Didn't I give you only support? Didn't I give you credit for knowing what you needed to do?"

"Kara, it sometimes seems as if your decision to leave Peter is based on our sexual relationship."

"That may have been the catalyst, but leaving Peter is something I thought about long before you returned home."

Danny felt shame. "Okay. I will support you. I won't say another discouraging word."

Kara said, "That was North Pine Lake Drive you just passed."

The road looked barely used. Weeds grew between cracks in the asphalt. A dented mailbox caught Danny's attention and she stopped the car. Breathing deeply, she glanced at Kara. "Are you game?"

And Kara asked, "Is this person dangerous?"

"He's a little strange, I guess. Mom said he lives back here in a shack without any electricity or plumbing."

Kara looked closely at her friend. "What you're saying is he could be hazardous to our health."

Danny nodded.

Kara shrugged. "Well, that never stopped us before, did it?"

The two-lane driveway penetrated a forest of Norway and white pines and tangled, scrub oak trees. It wound through the shaded woods in a serpentine fashion. Neither woman spoke. Grass and brush grazed the bottom and sides of the car. Danny realized she was holding her breath, and she glanced at Kara to see her staring intently through the windshield.

They jumped in unison when the shot sounded, but by then they had reached the shack. There was no way Danny could have backed the Escort out to the road; she would have to turn it around in order to escape with it.

A man carrying a shotgun approached the car. He wore a dirty T-shirt and torn overalls. "You ladies lost?" He peered in at Danny and she smelled burnt gunpowder. She noticed the lank, thinning hair hanging over his forehead, stared into skinny slate-colored eyes.

"I don't think so," she stammered, her heart hammering at her ribs.

He glanced at the gun and laughed, a barking sound that caused both women to jump again. "Just shooting at some crows," he explained.

Danny cleared her throat, knowing she would have to ask now because she couldn't do this again. She introduced herself and Kara and said, "I want to talk to you about buying some land."

Her attention focused on the building, which

wasn't really a shack. It looked like it had started out as a couple rooms and then been added to over the years. The materials used in construction didn't always go together, lending a rambling, disjointed air to the place. An electrical wire stretched across the clearing to the roof of the house. Two hound dogs were chained to a shed on the edge of the woods. She heard them barking, the sound rising to an almost hurtful howl and then dropping back into barks.

"You dogs hush up," he hollered and they dropped to the sandy earth and rested their heads on their paws.

"They listen well," Danny said, recalling Tipsy's uncontrollable barking. "I'm looking for a lot on the lake, Mr. Dupris. Thought you might sell me one with maybe a hundred feet of waterfront."

"Everyone wants a lot," he growled. "If I sold all them lots, I'd be rich but wouldn't have no privacy." He gestured toward the woods. "I start selling the land, won't be no place to run the dogs."

Danny felt Kara tug at her arm, heard her say, "We better be going then."

As the Escort snaked out the driveway, they heard the boom of the shotgun and the dogs barking.

Kara's face looked dark, almost angry. "I haven't been that scared in a long time."

Danny saw her enlarged pupils, the skin gone pale under her tan. "I'm sorry," she said dispiritedly. "I blew it."

"You left him your name and number. What more can you do? Short of falling on your knees and begging, which I don't think would make a damn bit of difference."

"You're probably right, but I wanted a place on that lake so much."

"Cottages and lakefront property sell all the time. We'll find something."

Danny brightened a little.

When she got home, only Tipsy was there to greet her. Tracy was still with her father at Roselawn. The house breathed quietly: a clock ticking, the refrigerator humming, the floors creaking.

Tipsy followed her to her room where he stretched out while she changed into sweats and T-shirt. "Want to go for a walk, doggy-o?"

Together they strolled toward the park. Streetlights, casting a yellow glow, held back the night. In the park Danny sat on a bench beyond the reach of any artificial lighting. She threw her head back and stared at the congregation of stars and galaxies, few of which she was ever able to identify.

"Hi." Chris's voice startled her, coming as it did from behind the bench.

Tipsy leaped to his feet with a startled woof, and Danny quieted him. "What brings you here?"

"Is it safe to sit next to you?"

"Sure. You scared him is all."

Chris let the dog sniff her hand as she sat on the bench and then patted him. "I was at Michael's. I think our work is done there."

"How did you happen to stop here?" Danny asked, wondering if Chris had followed her.

"I wanted to look at the river and then I saw

you. You're not with Kara tonight." Her face shadowed and unreadable, Chris leaned forward to look at Danny.

"I was with her. I haven't been home long."

"You never spend any evenings with me," Chris said softly.

Danny rested her arms on the back of the bench and told herself not to let it happen. It would be so easy.

"You'll be leaving the hardware store soon, won't you?"

Danny nodded. "I start working at the Tech in a couple weeks."

"Will I see you once in a while?" Chris's voice, always melodic, sounded almost imploring.

"When we can't play tennis anymore, maybe we can take up racquetball. Why don't we put aside a couple nights a week to do that."

Chris touched Danny's dangling hand. "Sounds like a plan."

Danny moved her hand away. "Don't waste your time on me, Chris. I don't even know what I want."

"Neither do I."

Chris startled her with a kiss, pinning her to the bench. Danny heard Tipsy's low, alarmed growls over the ringing in her ears and tried to pull away, but Chris drew her onto the grass and into the passion of the moment.

She felt Chris's hand reaching under her T-shirt to cup her breasts and listened to her soft laugh and sigh of pleasure when she slid a hand into Danny's shorts. Because of the heat, Danny wore no underwear. She envisioned those hands, strong and purposeful with blunt fingers, and she stiffened as she felt herself being entered, then moaned in answer to the gentle, coaxing rhythm.

It became an urgent contest, a wrestling match, a struggle between two physical equals. Danny ran a hand under Chris's shirt and over her smooth skin, feeling muscles taut and straining. She touched the full firm breasts, the solid ass, and plunged her hand into Chris's pants. Her fingers, intimately caressing, were drawn inside and held there.

They came quickly, almost at the same time. Lying still only long enough to catch her breath and gather her wits, Danny got up off the dry grass and pulled her clothes straight. She ran fingers through her hair and looked around to see if they had been seen. Apparently only Tipsy had witnessed their physical exchange. The park was deserted.

Chris stood up and rearranged her clothing. "Are you all right?" she asked, her teeth white in the shadow of her face.

Danny nodded. Shame washed over her. She couldn't even remember the descent to the earth. "I've got to go home." Her own voice sounded thick.

Chris grabbed her arm. "It doesn't have to be like this, you know."

Danny shook off the hand, suddenly fierce. "It should never be like this."

"Why don't you come to my apartment tomorrow night. I'll fix you dinner. We'll talk."

Danny laughed harshly. "No, thanks. Come on, Tips."

Chris walked next to her as Danny strode toward home. "I'm sorry. It just sort of happened."

"I know. It was my fault as much as yours. I'm not angry with you. I'm mad at myself."

"It's not fair. I never had a chance."

Danny realized the truth of what Chris said. "Nothing's fair."

Chris gave up trying to stop Danny's headlong rush toward home when Charlie passed them, tooting the Regal's horn.

After supper with Charlie and a brief exchange of talk, Danny fled to her room where she buried her face in her pillow and waited for the oblivion of sleep. Tomorrow she would deal with tonight. Maybe she would be less disgusted with herself then.

IX

Danny met Kara, as usual, at the Budget Inn after work Tuesday. Kara brought sandwiches, and Danny flopped on the double bed nearest the bathroom.

"I have to talk to you," Danny began. "Your husband called Monday, wanting to have lunch with me today." Wondering what he was going to say had added more worry to an already nerve-racking two days. She had spent Monday and Tuesday avoiding Chris, until Chris had cornered her Tuesday afternoon and told her that she only wanted to be friends, that she was sorry about what had happened in the park. Danny had accepted her words with relief and made a tennis date with her for Wednesday morning.

Kara's eyebrows shot toward her hairline. "And what did he have to say?"

"He said you're gone all the time, that you have no patience when you are home, that you're so different. What's going on, Kara? Do you have to make the man miserable?"

Kara sighed gustily. "And he wanted you to tell him why I'm different. Did you?"

"You know I didn't."

"I can't help it, Danny." Kara looked like she might cry. "I want out. I want my life back. I don't want to have dinner waiting for him every night or make love when he wants to make love or always do what he wants to do."

Danny scowled fiercely. "You sound like he never does anything on your terms."

"I usually mold my wants around his."

"Why?" Danny wanted to know.

"I don't know. Maybe because I thought that's the way it should be, because he brings home most of the money, because I have more time. Women's mentality." She leaned back into the pillows and took a bite out of her tuna on wheat. "Mmm. This is good."

Danny picked up her sub and bit into it. Hot peppers brought tears to her eyes and she reached for the shared can of pop. "What is women's mentality?"

"That we exist to please men, that men come first, that they're more important. I don't want to do that anymore." Kara choked a little and swallowed. "There's a listing for a lot on Pine Lake, north side too. I brought it with me."

"Let me see." Excitement shot through Danny as she reached for the print-out. "A hundred feet of frontage on the north side. Has to be near Dupris. This is too good to be true."

"You want to look at the place?"

"Oh, yes."

"How much will you give to see it?"

Danny took a last bite and licked her fingers, then tackled Kara who squealed and laughed as she toppled under Danny's weight.

They looked at the lake lot in the near dark, because Danny was unable to wait until the next day. Walking along the shoreline, they listened to the sounds of evening — soft wind soughing through the trees, tiny waves touching the beach, motors idling.

The land abutted Dupris' to the east, facing the sun all day and the warm southern breezes. Tall Norway pines, interspersed with white pines and scrub oaks, climbed the hill away from the shore. About a hundred feet or so from the water the hill leveled out.

Danny told Kara she would get up early in the morning for a second look and then decide whether to make an offer. She would have to cash in her bonds if it was accepted. They were all she had to fall back on now until the house was closed.

The next morning, as the sun rose over the east end of Pine Lake, she climbed through the trees to the hilltop. Needles underfoot softened her steps and made the going slippery, and she clutched for purchase at wild grape vines and tiny trees and bushes. At the high point, where the land stretched flat before her, there were only trees. She turned and watched the sunlight glitter on the water and wondered if she would be so lucky as to own this small piece of earth.

Loping down the hill, knowing she would be late for work, a shot rang overhead and a bullet lodged in a Norway pine — so close that she heard the thunk. She threw herself onto the bed of needles face first, her heart gone into a crazy erratic beat. It had to be Dupris. But why? Did she look like game?

He appeared at the top of the hill, just after his dogs swarmed over her. She had been certain, when she saw them snarling and barking as they scrambled down the hill toward her, that they were going to tear her apart. But here they were licking her face and whimpering. Spitting out acidy tasting pine needles, Danny rolled onto her back and tried to hold the overly affectionate dogs at bay.

"Git off her, you stupid dogs. Mack, Jimbo, come here." The dogs, tails still wagging, raced up the hill.

"You damn near killed me." Danny struggled to her feet and brushed herself clean of sand and needles. Indignantly, she awaited an explanation.

He simply said, "Thought you was a deer."

She was furious, hot with anger. "It's not deer hunting season."

"It's always deer hunting season," he said with an unashamed grin, which revealed gaps between long yellow teeth. "You ain't looking to buy this land, are you?" His eyes became suspicious slits.

"Maybe," she said somewhat defensively.

Grinning again, he said, "You sure you want me for a neighbor?"

"Your dogs are friendly, if you aren't."

Barking a laugh, he said, "It's one of their faults. Mack, Jimbo, come on." And he was gone, disappearing into the woods.

On the drive to the hardware store, she realized she'd better think hard about whether she wanted to live near a man who apparently shot at everything that moved — crows, coons, deer. It didn't matter the season.

Still shaken when she reached Morgan Hardware, she parked in the lot and walked through the already warm morning to the back door. The store had finally been affected by the long, hot spell. Without air conditioning, the heat had seeped through the ceiling and walls and windows, permeating the old building. The overhead fans lazily stirred it around, giving an illusion of coolness. This would be her last week here.

Stocking inventory on shelves, Chris called to her as she made her way to the check-out counter, and Danny realized she had missed their tennis game.

She hit her forehead with the heel of her hand. "I'm sorry, Chris. There was this little piece of land I wanted to see. That's all I could think of."

"I thought you slept in, but it's okay. It got me up and moving."

But it wasn't okay. Danny could see the hurt on Chris's face. "Want to play tomorrow morning instead?"

"Sure."

Danny called Kara in between customers. She

decided to let fate make the choice. If her offer was accepted, then she was meant to live near Dupris; if not, she would know it wasn't meant to be. But she knew she would feel terrible if she lost the chance to own the lot on Pine Lake. With all of her being, she wanted that bit of land, and in her mind she was already building the house.

"That land's been for sale before," Kara said, after hearing Danny out. "I think Dupris probably scared off all potential buyers. I'll worry about your safety if you get it."

Danny shrugged. "Maybe the offer won't be accepted."

"I'll bring the papers in for you to sign today."

Friday night Danny took Maureen out for fish. Friday night fish dinners were traditional in Wisconsin, dating to when Catholicism proscribed eating meat on that day of the week. Sitting across the table from Maureen, she gazed into the nearly black eyes that never ceased to hold her enthralled.

"Are you ready to start working at the Tech?" Maureen sipped white Zinfandel.

"I guess," Danny replied, tasting the salt rimming her margarita glass.

"Have you missed the challenge?"

"What challenge? Working with adults who lack English skills?"

Maureen looked annoyed. "There's a certain stimulation that comes from working with a faculty and administration of your peers."

"Sheer snobbery," Danny said, feeling contrary.

"No, it's not. I would think working in a hardware store would bore you."

"It offers endless diversity, and it requires imagination." Danny took a swig of the frothy drink.

"How's that?" Maureen's expression registered disbelief.

"People need help with their projects; they get ideas that need defining. You have to know a little about a lot of things — plumbing, electricity, carpentry."

"Fuck," Maureen said.

Danny laughed. "I like the pay at the Tech, though." Then she told Maureen about the land. "Did you ever want something so much you couldn't stand the thought of not getting it?" she asked and watched the lights in Maureen's eyes go out.

"Yes," she replied in the expressionless tone she reserved for her undisclosed past.

"What happened, Maureen, that was so awful?"

Maureen stared at her place setting as if lost in thought. When she spoke, her voice was so soft that Danny leaned forward to hear the words. "I loved her. I don't even know why. Maybe because I couldn't keep her."

"Tell me," she coaxed.

Maureen looked up and breathed deeply. "She received a job offer she said she couldn't refuse, and she didn't want me to go with her."

"Would you have gone with her?"

"We lived together nearly a year." She sounded flat.

"What was she like?" Danny asked, unable to imagine rejecting Maureen's love.

"A lot like you, as a matter of fact. Athletic, a little younger than I am. She wanted someone who enjoyed the things she wanted to do, or so she said." Maureen straightened, looking less dejected.

"Do you have any contact with her?"

"No, nor do I want any. We parted in anger."

Danny touched Maureen's hands, which were clasped tightly together on the tabletop. "It's never easy," she said, ready to share her memories of Rachel. But Maureen didn't appear to be listening.

As she always did, Danny left for home while Maureen slept. She longed to spend an entire night, waking and making love in the morning. It was hard to leave when Maureen's dark lashes graced her cheeks in sleep and her heavy hair spread over the pillow in lovely disarray. Tonight, when she looked down at the small, alabaster body, she felt that she knew a little more about Maureen and was closer to her because of it.

Late Saturday morning, Kara dropped in at the hardware store. She sought Danny with her eyes, even as she spoke to Chris and Brad. Danny lifted her eyebrows in question and Kara inclined her head in a nod. Elation swept through Danny.

"They accepted the offer?" she asked once they had a moment alone. She could barely believe her good luck.

"They did, sweetie. Hardly thought about it at all. They probably would have accepted it before now if they hadn't been out of town. Makes one wonder."

"I want to shout, Kara."

"Sure you can afford this, Danny?"

"I'll be cutting corners for a long time."

"We'll get you financing." Kara sounded confident.

Sunday, Danny showed the land to Tracy and Charlie. Tracy had returned from visiting her father a few days ago, and she looked a little bewildered.

Charlie eyed the hill from the beach and asked, "How did you pull this off?"

"Made an offer." Danny followed her mother's gaze, hoping Dupris wouldn't suddenly appear with Mack and Jimbo.

"I'd like it better without the hill," Charlie remarked.

"This whole side is hilly, Mom."

Charlie turned toward her daughter. "If you need some help, I have a little cash stored away I can lend you."

"Thanks, Mom, but I'll manage. How do you like it, Tracy?" she asked, thinking that next year Tracy would be off to college, would only be here during vacations.

"It's pretty," the girl conceded. "I'd have to have a car to live here, though."

Michael lifted his glass as he stood at the head of the table. "May we all be blessed with safe sex." Kara choked on her wine and he pounded her on the back. "You ought to think about it, sweetie. Lesbians are safer than anyone."

"I know." She met Danny's eyes and laughed.

Looking pleased, Michael sat down and cut his veal into little pieces.

Danny pushed the meat around her plate.

Michael eyed her with concern. "What's the

133

matter, honey? Don't you feel well? Something wrong with the food?"

"She probably doesn't eat veal," Tony said from the far end of the long table.

Danny glanced at him, then back at her plate. It would be rude to criticize the choice of food at their party.

"Sweetie, we know all about the little calves. We hardly ever touch veal either, but this is a special occasion." Michael took a small taste and chewed, encouraging Danny to do the same.

She laughed and took a bite. Here wasn't the place to make a statement.

Danny and Kara sat across from each other next to Michael. Chris and Maureen flanked Tony. In the table's midsection sat Kevin and Mark and the guests of the house.

Chris said, "I grew up on a farm. It's hard to make ends meet. You do what you have to do. We didn't raise calves for veal, though, just sold off some of the young stock."

"I didn't know you were a farm girl, Chris," Kara remarked with interest.

"The roots of society," Mark interjected.

"Well, if that's true, the roots are in trouble," Chris replied dryly.

"I think we're all in a mire," Kevin remarked. "We can't get decent funding for a disease that's epidemic."

Danny said, "You know, there's a place like this in Roselawn. I spent a lot of time there. I wondered if you'd heard of that buddy house?" She glanced at Michael and Tony.

"Nope, not that one. I've heard of others. Was it

successful?" Michael asked, looking at her with interest.

"I thought so. Oh, there were problems but they got ironed out."

"Well, we're doing our bit. And we want to thank you all for helping us make our idea a reality." Michael smiled.

"Let's have some cheer." Tony raised his wine glass. "To success in our new venture."

"*Prosit,*" Kevin said, hoisting his nearly empty glass.

Maureen looked amused. "I want to commend the cooks. I couldn't have done better myself."

They moved from the dining room to the library with its walnut-paneled walls and shelves of books. The heat wave had broken just before Labor Day weekend, and a fire pulsed in the fireplace. Danny studied the titles, wondering where they all came from.

"I called you three nights in a row before I finally gave up," Michael said, filling her empty glass.

"I've been working nights." Classes had started at the Tech, and Danny taught Monday and Wednesday nights as well as part of every weekday. Tuesday nights she spent at the Budget Inn with Kara, Friday and Saturday nights with Maureen. Small wonder he hadn't reached her.

"I hear you bought some land," Tony said, handing her a plate with cheesecake on it. "Keep us in mind if you're going to build. We'll want to help."

"Thanks."

Kara told everyone about their meeting with Dupris, about the shot he had taken at Danny.

It caused Danny to ask, "How are *your* neighbors?"

Michael rolled his eyes. "Curious. I think they think we've got a commune going. This woman knocked on the door yesterday with a casserole. I know she wanted me to invite her in. She said a bed and breakfast was a wonderful idea and she would pass the word."

"Did you tell her what kind of bed and breakfast you're running?" Kara asked. "She might send you heterosexual guests."

"She'll catch on."

The buzzing in Danny's ears continued all evening. When at last she stood on Maureen's porch awaiting admittance, she remarked, "Nice evening."

Maureen gave her a quizzical look. "I enjoyed it." Once inside, she said, "I'm going to bed. Coming?"

"You don't have to ask twice." Removing her clothes and heaping them on a chair, she helped Maureen off with hers. "I love taking your clothes off. You have the most beautiful body."

"Well, yours isn't exactly ugly."

"Is that supposed to be a compliment?" Danny gently pushed her onto the bed and collapsed next to her.

Maureen laughed, a husky sound. "You know you have a nice body."

"I don't think I'm up to this tonight." Danny felt as if her arms weighed too much to move.

"That's okay with me."

They fell asleep on top of the bedspread, wrapped around each other.

The bedside clock pointed to two-thirty when

136

Danny awakened and padded to the bathroom. Her head ached dully and her mouth felt dry as dust. When she returned, she pulled the blankets back and covered them both. Maureen stirred and murmured, and Danny felt the beginnings of desire.

Ignoring Maureen's attempts to return to sleep, she caressed her into passion. The mind created this sexual hunger, she thought. But why Maureen? Why did she have such a need for this woman? It mystified her.

Danny slept late Sunday morning, having reluctantly left Maureen's bed for her own. The day blew a cold north wind across overcast skies; she heard it rustling the ash tree and rattling the windows whenever she awakened. The phone she had ordered for her bedroom rang, rousing her from an unpleasant dream, and Kara's voice filled her ear.

"I need to talk to you. Peter and I had the most awful fight."

"What time is it, Kara?"

"Late. After nine-thirty."

There were tears in Kara's voice and Danny pulled herself up on an elbow. "What happened?"

"I can't tell you over the phone."

"Well, come on over then. Just give me time to take a quick shower."

Dressed in sweats, her thick hair still wet, Danny let Kara in the back door. Only Tipsy had greeted her when she got out of bed. He had been lying outside her bedroom door. She put him in the fenced-in backyard.

"Sorry to wake you up like that, but I was desperate to talk to you."

"Sit down. I'll make some coffee."

Kara removed her coat and threw it over a chair, then sat at the kitchen table.

"Want some breakfast?"

"No, thanks. Where is everyone?"

"Beats me. I'm feeling like a very bad mother these days. No one's ever home." She plunked into a chair while the water dripped through the ground beans and turned into coffee. "You look exhausted." And Kara did. There were dark sacks under her blue eyes. Danny swallowed a yawn. "Talk to me."

"Peter lit into me last night for being gone so much. I can't blame him." Kara absently ran a hand over the top of the table as if wiping it clean. She looked pleadingly at Danny. "I told him if he didn't like it to find someone else. Can you believe it?" Tears hovered on the edge of her lower lids and ran down her cheeks. It looked like the blue was running out of her eyes.

Thinking that no one ever looked as sad as Kara did when she cried, Danny reached for the hand wiping at the tears. "Now what?"

"We're going to counseling. What am I going to tell a counselor? That I'm having an affair with a woman?" Kara sniffed and laughed bleakly.

"Well, not when Peter's there anyway."

"I need comforting. Let's go to your room." Her smile shimmered among the tears.

"Not here. We'll go to the lake or someplace. Are Tuesdays out?"

"I live for Tuesdays," Kara said with feeling.

They drove to Pine Lake County Park and sat in the Escort which rocked slightly in the cold wind. It was an unfriendly day. Tipsy panted from the back seat, eager to be released. Finally, they got out and walked the beach. No one else was at the park or on the lake. To get to Danny's property they would have to walk along Dupris' shore and Kara refused to do that. She had let Danny know her horror at everything she had heard about and seen of Dupris.

"Danny, I'm not sure I want to live next door to that man."

"You don't have to, Kara. The property isn't even bought, the house isn't built, you haven't left Peter, and you're worried about living next to Dupris?" Danny tucked her head into her collar, turned her back against the cold wind and shivered.

Staring at the gray waves, Kara also stood hunched with the wind at her back. "I don't know what I'd do if something happened to you. I think I'd lose my mind."

"What could happen to me?" She called Tipsy to her and praised him for coming.

"We could both die from exposure. Apparently, we don't have sense enough to get out of the cold."

Shifting from one foot to the other, Danny talked about what a sentence had to have to be complete. Her feet hurt in new shoes. She wore a skirt and blazer today. The crotch of her pantyhose didn't reach the joining of her legs, a familiar problem for her because of her long legs, and she felt somewhat hobbled. She longed to kick off the shoes and hike up the pantyhose. Distracted and irritated, she struggled to keep her mind on her job and her tone friendly.

When she could, Danny stepped out in the hallway and, glancing up and down and seeing no one, tugged at the crotch of her pantyhose and felt it rip. "Damn," she hissed, wishing herself back at the hardware store. At least there she had never worn skirts or dresses and, therefore, no pantyhose. Returning to the classroom, where the fifteen students were working on a writing assignment, she sat at her desk and slid her feet out of her shoes. She read and corrected papers she had requested from the previous class, appalled at the butchering of the English language, even by those who had been born in this country and attended its schools. Her red marking pen flashed across the pages without mercy. When there was improvement, though, she praised it well.

After the students dribbled out of the classroom, Danny stuffed papers into her briefcase and shut the door behind her. She walked down the hall, hoping Maureen might be working late but knowing she probably would be gone for the day.

She had seen little of Maureen at work, especially on the days she taught into the evenings. When she had eight a.m. classes, Maureen was usually already busy by the time Danny arrived at school. Sometimes they had coffee or ate together in the cafeteria, but often a whole work week went by when they only greeted each other in passing. She found Maureen's office door closed and locked.

Buttoning her coat, she stepped out through the double doors and hurried toward her car. Crisp and cold, the night greeted her and she filled her lungs with it. She had been inside for ten hours. Brown, curled leaves skittered across the sidewalk before the wind. Throwing her head back, she looked at the black, starry sky. Scudding clouds briefly blocked out portions of galaxies and whole constellations. It was nearly the end of October. Next year, she thought, she'd be driving to her home on Pine Lake.

A light over the sink lit her way into the kitchen. She looked into the refrigerator, opened a can of Seven-Up and took it to her room. The house was quiet but not empty. Tracy and Charlie and Tipsy must have gone to bed.

There were no lights seeping out into the upstairs hallway. When Danny flipped the switch in her room, she saw Tracy curled up asleep on her bed, the bedspread doubled back over her slender body. The girl's eyelids fluttered and opened, and she covered her eyes.

"Sorry, sweetie. I didn't know you were here." Danny switched on the bedside lamp and turned off the overhead fixture.

Tracy rolled onto her back and stretched. "Hi, Mom. How was school?"

Smiling, Danny replied, "Okay. How was your school?"

"I made the A honor roll." Tracy sat up and grinned at her mother. She looked sleepy — hair and clothes rumpled, cheeks pink, eyes glazed.

Delighted, Danny clapped her hands together. "Wonderful, Tracy. I'm so proud of you. You know, it's time to do something about college."

"I got some application forms for U.W. Madison. Kim is applying there too."

"Good," Danny said, hiding sudden worry. Was

Tracy ready for the freedom? There would be no one to urge her to study, to eat, to sleep. The lack of boundaries might cause her failure.

"Dad said he'd pay my tuition if you'd pay room and board. I was supposed to tell you that. I can work too, you know."

"You can work next summer," Danny agreed, removing her clothes, peeling off the offending pantyhose with a sigh of relief. "They're never long enough."

"I know. On me the legs end mid-thigh and every time I bend over they start sliding off my butt."

It hadn't occurred to Danny that Tracy, of course, would have the same problem. Her legs were as long as Danny's. They now looked each other in the eye.

Tracy got up off the bed. "Grandma thinks I should apply for financial aid. Can we fill out forms tomorrow night?"

"Sure."

"I suppose you'll be out Friday and Saturday nights, anyway." Tracy eyed her mother with interest. "What do you do until three or four in the morning?"

An involuntary flush crept up Danny's neck and suffused her face. "Talk."

"Come on, Mom. Until three or four in the morning every weekend?"

Danny searched for a reasonable explanation but thought of none. Laughter burbled up her throat and she pushed it back down. "We have some interesting conversations."

"Why don't you just stay there overnight?"

Danny smiled a little. "Maybe I should. Now let's go to bed. I'm glad you waited for me to get home. I really am proud of you, sweetie." She leaned forward and kissed Tracy on the cheek.

X

Late on a Saturday, Danny gazed at the lake from her hilltop property. She had walked in from the road, marking a course for a driveway.

The divorce was complete. She was a single person, and she felt rotten — lost in a sea of memories. She had thought this was what she wanted, and she didn't understand her reaction to the settlement check and the court papers. Instead of elation, she felt melancholy and strangely restless.

Plunging her hands deep in her jeans pockets, she squinted at the chilly blue water and sky. The

November wind lifted her hair and probed her scalp with cold fingers. She wore a heavy jacket with a sweater under it, but the icy touch of winter reached through her clothes and her apathy and caused her to shiver. It reminded her of the bleak months ahead.

She had turned forty in August, and today she thought she was on the launching pad of old age with nothing to mark the passing years. Was this the onset of midlife crisis? She had failed at marriage, had done Craig a disservice by marrying him, was now indecisive in love, only moderately successful at motherhood, and no more advanced in a career than she had been when she left Roselawn.

Thinking of her fortieth birthday, which only she and Tracy and Charlie had celebrated on the designated date, she grimaced. She had sworn Kara to silence, when Kara had wanted to tell Michael and Tony and Chris. Instead, Kara had taken her to lunch and given her a thick, gold chain. Danny had protested the cost and Kara said she had spent commission money. Maureen had fixed her a dinner and given her a sexy blouse and shorts. It looked like something Maureen would wear, rather elegant.

Stamping her feet against the hard ground, she attempted to warm them. She had deposited the settlement check on the way out of town. She could now think about building and had already looked into a log house. But she would be in debt forever once she closed on the land and obtained the financing to start construction. Was this what she wanted? She wasn't sure, now that it remained just out of her grasp, a very real possibility.

Tipsy shook against her leg, his brown curls

straightening in the breeze. The pines moaned, swaying in the wind. Half an hour later, when the sun began its quick descent toward the horizon, she climbed gratefully into the Escort and pointed it toward home.

For the first time since the beginning of their love affair, Danny didn't feel any inner urge to hurry to Maureen's. She showered and changed slowly, ready to leave the house as Charlie came home from working at the IGA.

"Don't worry if I don't come home tonight, Mom. I may spend the night at a friend's. Tracy won't be home either. She's at Kim's."

"That so?" Charlie flopped into a kitchen chair and reached for the calf of one leg. "I'll have a quiet night home with the dog for company."

But Danny thought she looked and sounded disappointed. "I don't have to rush off. I can sit and talk awhile."

"I heard some gossip at the store you maybe should know about. Probably nothing to it."

"What gossip, Mom?" Danny sat down, too, and looked into her mother's eyes for a clue.

Charlie massaged her leg. "Well, I thought you might be interested since it's about Kara. I heard she's leaving her husband."

"Who'd you hear that from?"

"A neighbor of hers, belongs to the same country club. Is Peter fooling around?"

Danny kept her face blank. "I don't think so."

"Is Kara?"

"If I knew that, Mom, I wouldn't tell."

"Sounds like yes."

"No, it doesn't. Kara's my best and oldest friend. Don't go gossiping about her."

"I wouldn't. I'm very fond of Kara. She always seemed a little flighty, though."

Danny scowled fiercely, as angry at Kara as at her mother. Was Kara moving out without telling her? She surely would have said something Tuesday night. Instead, she had talked about the counselor she and Peter were seeing — a woman who was a sex therapist. This was not such a small town anymore that everyone was food for talk, but Kara had lived here all her life and a lot of people knew her. She would ask her when she saw her. She got up. "Will you be lonely?"

Charlie scoffed. "Me? Lonely? I'll watch some TV and read. It'll be nice and quiet." Danny bent and kissed her mother's soft cheek. She appreciated the carefully guarded independence, the unassuming attitude behind the brash front. "See you tomorrow."

"Aren't you taking an overnight bag?"

Danny lifted a paper sack. "It's all in here. I don't need much." Mentally, she reviewed the contents: a toothbrush and toothpaste, some shampoo and conditioner and a razor, a change of underwear and socks and sweats. She reminded herself that it was possible Maureen wouldn't want her to stay overnight, but how she hated leaving that warm bed in the middle of the night for the chilly ride home.

Sitting on Maureen's couch a short time later, Danny thought she should have stayed home instead of bringing this mood to Maureen's. Nevertheless, she voiced her thoughts. "Do you ever feel as if your life has amounted to diddly squat?" Slouching, she stretched her long legs out in front of her, crossing them at the ankles.

Maureen had just brought them each a glass of wine and looked at her with questioning eyes. "No. Why?" She sat next to Danny and crossed her legs.

"Was there no time in your life when you felt everything was pointless?" Danny clasped her hands behind her head.

"What is wrong with you?"

Gazing at the black eyes, Danny looked for some understanding. "Tell me about yourself, Maureen, about your growing up."

"That's all history." Maureen sounded impatient and made a dismissive gesture.

"But you never talk about the past. It's the past that made us what we are. When you went to Indiana who did you visit?"

"I told you. My sister and her family." She smiled humorlessly. "I have two sisters, one brother, seven nieces and nephews. My father and another brother died in the coal mines." She sat silent for a moment, then continued, "I prayed from the time I turned eleven that my father would die in a cave-in or explosion, but not my brother."

The words shocked Danny into stillness.

"My father started reaching into my underwear when I turned eleven. He slugged my brothers whenever they dared to disagree with him. I think he thought we were his property, like the dishes or the car or my mother." Her voice sounded brittle. "I found out later that he did the same to my sisters, that they were glad when he died too."

Danny hadn't expected her questions to elicit

such a disturbing response. She recalled her own father, kind and gentle and quiet, felled by a massive heart attack at fifty-five. She had felt cheated, knowing at twenty-eight that she would never have a meaningful conversation with him. She had not known how to start one. She cleared her throat. "And your mother?"

Maureen laughed harshly. "I told her once and she slapped me and told me not to tell dirty lies. I seldom see my mother. She married again."

Danny slipped an arm around Maureen's shoulders. "I'm sorry," she said, not knowing what else to say.

Maureen went on as if Danny hadn't spoken. "I escaped, though. One of my sisters got herself pregnant and married before she graduated from high school, a miserable marriage just to get away. My other sister landed a secretarial job in Indianapolis. And I won a scholarship and went on to college. My oldest brother joined the military, the other went into the mines. I think the brother who went into the mines stuck around to try to protect us girls at home. He was killed in the same accident as my father. A mixed blessing but too late for us kids."

Danny remained silent. It was as if Maureen had forgotten her anyway.

"My mother mourned my father. I couldn't believe it. He had knocked her around as much as anyone."

Danny pulled Maureen close. She felt worse for knowing Maureen's past. She wondered if people went through the same agenda when they turned forty as they had at twenty. Did they wonder about purpose and worth and failure? Or did they just want to capture the joy of living before they lost their looks and health?

During the night, Danny awakened and glanced at the clock. She even started to drag herself out of bed and then remembered. She was sleeping over, just as Tracy slept over at Kim's. Did the two girls make love as she had earlier with Maureen?

She hadn't intended to make love that night, had thought Maureen wouldn't want to be touched sexually after remembering her youth. But Maureen had started the lovemaking. It had been quiet and intense and more passionate than usual.

The morning sun in Danny's eyes and a full bladder brought her out of a sluggish dream. She rolled out of bed and padded to the bathroom, then went to the kitchen for a drink of water. Glancing out the window at the pale day, she thought about last night's revelation. It was difficult to imagine Maureen, who seemed almost arrogant, as a victim.

Returning to the bedroom she slid between the sheets and pulled herself up tight against Maureen's backside. Straightening Maureen's dark curls between her fingers, she watched them bounce back. She massaged Maureen's back for a long time, gently working her way toward the small bottom. Once there she slid her hand between her legs.

Maureen tensed and moaned a little, but Danny thought she had been awake from the first touch. She rolled Maureen onto her back. "How do you want it?" she asked, as she might have asked Kara. "Sunny side up, over easy, omelet style?"

Maureen sounded and looked annoyed. "Why do you ask?"

"Thought you might have a preference."

"I don't think I want it at all." Maureen pushed herself to a sitting position. "I think I'd like coffee."

"Okay," Danny said, swallowing disappointment. "I'll go make it for you."

"You don't have to do that."

"I want to." She started to get up but Maureen pulled her back.

"Upside down," she said.

Feeling a spurt of hot excitement, Danny let herself be drawn into it.

It was Tuesday before Danny relayed Charlie's gossip to Kara.

Kara responded angrily, "I never told anyone except you that I was thinking about leaving Peter. Maybe Peter *is* fooling around." She sounded indignant. "I'll cut his goddamn balls off."

"How can you do that when you're cheating on him?"

"That's different."

"How?"

"I'm cheating with a woman."

"Oh, Kara, talk about splitting hairs. You promised to tell me about your counseling sessions. Remember?"

"For bodily payment."

"Later," Danny said with a laugh.

"Actually, they're not that interesting. We don't need the sex therapy. It's too late for me. I want to talk to her alone."

"Are you just going through the motions?"

"Maybe. I don't know."

They had shoved Danny's log house plans onto the floor and lay with arms and legs wrapped around each other, their breathing and heartbeats slowing to normal — breasts and bellies and lips touching.

"How aerobic is this, do you think?" Kara murmured.

"I doubt if anyone's gotten skinny doing it," Danny replied, gently kissing Kara's soft lips.

"Too bad. I could really get into this. What a wonderful way to lose weight."

"Where does Peter go on Tuesday nights?"

"He thinks it's girls night out, which it is," Kara whispered back.

"I like Peter."

"I like him too. I wish I didn't. All this would be a hell of a lot easier if I didn't care about him." Kara breathed a sigh into Danny's mouth.

"Are you going to move out?"

"How else am I going to find out what I do want. I'm making everyone miserable this way."

"Will you take the kids with you?"

"If they'll come." Kara pulled away and rolled onto her back.

"Maybe you should wait until the kids go off to college."

"I might lose you."

"You should be so lucky."

Danny dressed swiftly. They were running late as

usual, unwilling to end the evening. She shrugged into her suit jacket and looked over at Kara as she brushed her hair into its static halo.

Kara leaned forward to apply lipstick. "I hear Tracy has a boyfriend."

"Who told you that?"

"Laura. His name is Scott and he's a track star, tall and skinny and cute."

"She hasn't mentioned him to me."

"Mothers are the last to know. Laura broke up with Steve, thank God, and I didn't know for weeks."

"I don't know why kids want to go steady. It's too much like marriage."

Kara looked at Danny from her reflection. "It gives them a sense of security. They feel wanted and they're assured of a date."

Danny hugged Kara from behind. "You'll never lose me, Kara. I love you too much."

"I wasn't referring to friendship. I know we'll always be friends." She kissed Danny lightly, careful not to mark her with lipstick. "Come on, sweetie. It's time to go home. When you build that house, maybe I'll take vacations with you."

"And we'll have a place of our own for Tuesday nights."

Finding Tracy and the dog curled up on the couch together in front of the television set, Danny ordered Tipsy to the floor. "You know he's not allowed on the furniture."

"He likes to be comfy too." Tracy tore her eyes from the TV and looked at her mother. "Where do you go Tuesday nights?"

"I've told you, I go out with Kara."

"Where, though?"

Danny shrugged and sat on the davenport. "Out to eat and talk. I hear you have a boyfriend."

Tracy made a face, rolling her eyes and sighing. "He's just a friend."

"I want to meet him if you're going out with him," Danny persisted.

"Okay, Mom. If we go on an official date, you'll meet him." She turned back to the program she had been watching. "Chris called you."

Danny dialed Chris's number and sat on a nearby chair to remove her shoes. "What's up?" she asked when Chris came on the line.

"Thought I better tell you I sprained my ankle yesterday, putting softener salt in some lady's car. Tripped going down those back steps at the store. I won't be able to play racquetball Thursday night."

"Are you working tomorrow?"

"No, not tomorrow, but I may work a few hours Thursday. I've got a bad case of cabin fever already."

"Can I help out any? Pick up something for you?"

"The cupboard will be bare by Thursday," Chris said slowly.

"What do you need? I'll swing by the store Thursday and get some groceries."

"Maybe I'll be okay by then."

"I have to grocery shop anyway," Danny said. She met Charlie at the IGA once a week and together they stocked up on food and staples. "It's better you let the ankle heal." Working at the hardware store would cause it enough stress, she knew, remembering how her legs sometimes ached after standing on them all day.

* * * * *

Wednesdays turned into such long days. Already worn out before her night class began, Danny sat in the cafeteria with Michael and Maureen. She looked at the greasy chicken cordon bleu and dried heap of rice on her plate, the miserably small salad already turning brown in its plastic bowl, and her appetite shriveled.

"Remember the lady who came to the door with the casserole? Well, her husband's causing trouble," Michael said, glancing at Danny. "It's not veal, sweetie. Eat. You're getting thin."

"You should talk," she said. His body defined the word thin.

He pushed his winter-darkening red hair away from his high, pale forehead impatiently. "You look tired, Danny."

She knew she did. She awoke nights and couldn't go back to sleep, worrying as she did about so many things: Tracy leaving home for the university next fall, money, Dupris and his guns and dogs, money, the implications inherent in loving two women, money, the possibility of Kara leaving Peter, money. She disliked feeling anxious about every dollar spent. The difficulty, she thought, lay in knowing that she was about to make a lifetime financial commitment without anyone to share it with her.

She ignored his concern and asked, "What kind of trouble?"

"This guy checked our credentials for running a bed and breakfast, and we're legal. There's no problem with that. But we don't have any license authorizing us to care for sick people."

"Do you need one?" Maureen asked.

"Well, technically maybe. Depends on how you look at our AIDS guests, I suppose. We don't provide them with nursing home care, but some do need extra attention. We can't have ambulances galloping in and out all the time, and we can't be running our guests to immediate care constantly, either. I don't know." He sounded discouraged. "We'll just do our best."

"That's all anyone can do." Danny shrugged.

"So, how do you like working at the Tech?" he asked, changing the subject.

"I like this part of it, having dinner with you two."

"She preferred working at the hardware store, if you can believe that." Maureen cocked one thin eyebrow and shrugged in apparent disbelief.

"Oh, I can understand that," Michael said with a grin. "I think hardware stores are fascinating, and most of the customers are men."

"Well, you're two of a kind then." She stood up and gathered her empty dishes and utensils.

Danny remembered Chris. "Chris sprained her ankle carrying softener salt to someone's car. I'm going to take her some groceries tomorrow. I won't have time today."

"Well, give her my regards. Got to go now. I'll see you both tomorrow."

As Maureen disappeared through the double doors of the cafeteria, Michael said, "You two have a thing going, don't you?"

Smiling slightly, Danny nodded.

"Does she know about Kara?"

"Do you?"

"I know something's going on between you and Kara."

Sighing, Danny leaned her elbows on the table and rested her chin on the heel of one hand.

His green eyes glowed from under thick red lashes. "That works for a while," he said quietly.

Danny might have argued with him last summer. Now she felt more inclined to agree with him. "I don't know what to do about it."

"I just hope no one gets hurt too badly." His penetrating gaze unsettled her. "Think I should call on Chris tonight?"

"I'm sure she'd be happy to see you," Danny said.

"I'll do it, then." He squeezed Danny's shoulder. "Sweetie, I've done that scene with two or more lovers more than once. Logically, it should work. Practically, it doesn't. After a while, it's hard to keep it up." He grinned devilishly at his pun. "Seriously, though, someone always gets jealous, and you spread yourself too thin trying to please everyone and satisfy no one. Eventually you have to make a choice."

"You're making me feel terrific," she remarked dryly, feeling drained and depressed instead.

"Well, on the other hand, maybe it'll work for you."

Danny leaned forward, wanting to confide in him, but then changed her mind.

"What?" he asked.

"Nothing." She noticed the time. "Now I've got to go. Class starts in twenty minutes."

* * * * *

At the IGA Thursday afternoon Danny trudged up and down the aisles with Charlie, throwing food and staples into the cart, separating Chris's purchases from her own.

"Who's getting that stuff?" Charlie asked.

"Chris sprained her ankle. I told her I'd pick up some food for her."

"Isn't she the one you played tennis with?"

"Yep. We switched to racquetball not long ago." Danny tossed a box of cereal into her own part of the basket.

Charlie glanced at Danny curiously. "I heard some talk about her."

"You're turning into the town gossip, you know that, Mom?"

"I won't tell you then." Charlie turned into the next aisle and put some toilet paper into the cart.

Danny felt her face settling into lines of disapproval and thought that if her mother was turning into a gossip, she was a bit of a prude about it. What could be wrong with exchanging news? "What did you hear?"

"I've heard this more than once," she whispered confidentially. "She's a homosexual."

Annoyed because her heart beat a faster tattoo, Danny snapped, "Oh, Mom, so what?"

"Forewarned is forearmed, that's what."

"You're warning me?" The absurdity of it caused Danny to laugh. Leaning on the cart handle, she guffawed until she thought she would wet her pants. Sobering, she drew a deep breath and straightened.

Charlie wore an expression of uncertainty, as if she thought the joke might be on her. "What is so funny?"

"Nothing, Mom. Let's finish and get out of here."

They loaded the back end of the Escort and drove home through the dark streets. Danny carried in the groceries, then delivered Chris her purchases.

Chris met her at the door. While the two of them talked, Danny put away the groceries, fixed Chris something to eat, put ice on her ankle and rewrapped it.

"Michael showed up last night. He made me eat a sandwich," Chris said, her gray eyes huge and dark in a pale face in which every freckle stood out. "Will I see you tomorrow? "

"I'll come after work for a little while," Danny promised before leaving.

Sleet spewed out of the overcast sky, stabbing her face with icy fingers. She shivered and slipped on the already slick street. Unlocking her car, she threw her purse onto the passenger seat and slid behind the wheel, slamming the door shut behind her.

At home, Danny filled a plate and joined Tracy and Charlie at the kitchen table.

"Tracy has a date Friday night," Charlie said.

Danny turned to look at her daughter. "Am I going to meet him?"

"Yep, if you're home around seven. But you always go out on weekends."

"With some woman," Charlie muttered.

"Well, I don't see you bringing home any men, Mom," Danny said unkindly. "I'll be home."

The following afternoon Chris met her at the door with crutches and a grin. "They rent these at the hardware store."

"I know. I worked there too. Remember?"

Easing herself onto the couch, Chris patted the cushion next to her. "Seems like a long time ago. Sit down."

Danny took a seat in a chair next to the sofa. "I can't stay long. I have to be home to meet Tracy's date."

"That's okay. One of your students is coming over."

"Who?"

"Tina Sanjinis." Danny looked dumbfounded and Chris explained, "I do some tutoring on the side. I guess I never told you that. Actually, this will be the first time I work with her. What's she like?"

"Shy, quiet, like most of the Chicanas I have in class."

"Maybe they're that way because of the way you are."

Danny snorted. "What do you mean?"

"You're tall, you're commanding, you're knowledgeable, you're attractive. That all adds up to intimidating."

Danny grew quiet, wondering if any of that was true. She met Chris's eyes. "You look better. How's the ankle?"

"I feel better. If you have time over the weekend, come see me."

"Do you need anything?" Danny stood up. She hadn't removed her coat.

Chris's gray eyes warmed with a smile. "Just company every once in a while."

* * * * *

Tracy snapped at her mother and grandmother while she picked at the food Danny insisted she eat. "Mom, I'm not hungry. Why do I have to eat? You're not eating."

"Just a little something to keep your strength up," Charlie soothed.

"I was talking to Mom, Grandma."

"This isn't the Prince of Wales you're going out with, you know. You don't have to be afraid of him," Charlie snapped back.

"I'm not afraid of anyone." Tracy jumped to her feet.

"Calm down, will you two?" If Tracy was going to be like this before every date, Danny thought, she would drive Charlie and herself away and maybe the boy, too. "It's perfectly natural to be uptight, sweetie, but you don't have to be rude. Why don't you just go get ready?"

Tracy threw her napkin onto the table. "Fine. If you don't want me here, I can take a hint." She flipped her head, tossing the kinky strands outward, and marched out of the kitchen.

"Well," Charlie said, her eyes flashing with unexpected humor, "I don't envy that young man."

"She's just a little nervous, Mom."

"I know, honey. I don't remember you ever being that way, though, but then you didn't date until college, did you?"

Danny remembered. She hadn't wanted to date boys. She smiled enigmatically.

"You were so cute, too." Charlie's eyes narrowed and Danny thought she might be putting two and two together, but she came up with three. "Well, that's all water under the bridge. You going out with what's-her-name tonight?"

"Maureen, you mean? Yes."

"Are you coming home to sleep?"

Danny tensed. "Probably not."

Danny got up to answer the doorbell, while Charlie restrained the barking dog. Almost no one entered the house through the front door, and she had to tug on it to get it open. A tall, skinny boy with a slight stoop stood in the opening. "You must be Scott. Come on in."

He sat on the couch, waiting for Tracy to appear. His eyes and hair were a deep brown, his mouth and cheeks cherry red, his face long with a squarish chin. He looked wholesome and harmless.

Maureen and Danny ate downtown. Danny had no wish to go to the mall and possibly run into Scott and Tracy, who were going to a movie. Tracy would think she was checking up on her. Danny chose Anthony's where she and Maureen had gone on their first date.

They were seated in a booth under a false arbor laced with artificial grapes. Danny toyed with her drink. "When we were in Roselawn, Tracy dated a boy in her class. It's funny she hasn't dated anyone else until now." She laughed a little. "I even thought maybe she was gay."

Maureen's black eyes flashed. "She could be gay. Didn't you date? I did. Would it bother you if she was gay?"

Danny gave the question serious consideration. "I don't think so," she replied, then said lightly, "I wouldn't have any grandchildren."

"You might. More and more single women are choosing to have children."

"What's wrong?" Danny asked, meeting the measuring gaze.

Maureen set her wine glass down. "Donna is coming for a visit."

Perplexed, Danny asked, "Donna who?"

"Donna was my last lover."

"Oh," Danny said stupidly, a flush spreading over her skin. "You never told me her name." She recalled Maureen telling her that she, Danny, reminded Maureen of her last lover. "When?"

"Tomorrow morning."

Danny's eyes felt like burnt holes in the heat of her face. "I guess I better not spend the night with you."

Maureen smiled tightly. "Yes, you should."

"You want me to make her jealous, is that it?"

The smile vanished. Maureen's eyes became flat. "I didn't say that. I didn't ask her to come. She didn't ask me if I wanted her to visit. She just said she'd be at the apartment Saturday morning. I'm not changing anything for her."

Danny sat in sullen silence waiting for their dinner to arrive. Then, realizing she was being churlish, she made an effort to brighten. "I saw Chris this afternoon."

"How's she doing?"

"Better. She's not very mobile and she gets lonely."

"We should have her over for dinner tomorrow night."

Was Maureen tired of being alone with her? "Is Donna coming to dinner too?"

"I haven't asked her. The post card she sent announced her arrival, nothing more — like royalty."

When they climbed into bed that night, they were still at odds with each other. Danny, who couldn't put her finger on why she felt slightly betrayed, thought lovemaking might close the gap between them.

"What's wrong?" Maureen asked, sounding accusatory.

"What do you mean?"

"You're dry as a bone."

Danny recognized the feel of it. This had happened occasionally with Craig and once with Kara. She didn't want it told to her, though, especially not by Maureen. She rolled Maureen onto her back. "Let me make love to you."

XI

Opening her eyes to daylight, Danny nudged
Maureen. "Someone's at the door." After Maureen left
the room, she heard her talking to someone, listened
to their voices move through the apartment.
Reluctantly, she rolled out of bed and padded to the
bathroom where she looked at herself in the
mirrored shower door while peeing. Her hair stood in
disarray. She would meet no one without a shower.

Dressed in sweats, her hair still wet, Danny
found herself rendered nearly speechless by Donna's
looks. Tall, big-boned, handsome, with startling light

blue eyes and blondish hair, Donna was a knockout. After the introduction, Danny looked questioningly at Maureen. She had expected a physical resemblance between herself and Donna and realized, on reflection, that Maureen hadn't claimed any.

"Would you pick up Chris for dinner tonight?"

"Sure," Danny said absently, sneaking a glance at Donna's sensuous mouth with sinking hopes. The woman was gorgeous, an athletic goddess. No wonder Maureen had been devastated by losing her.

Danny had poured herself a cup of coffee but had no thirst for it. She leaned against the kitchen counter, wanting to flee. She should go home anyway and inquire about Tracy's evening. She put her cup down abruptly. "I've got things to do. I'll see you both tonight. I'll call Chris and see if she wants a lift, Maureen." She hesitated, then kissed Maureen on the cheek.

"I thought you were staying for breakfast," Maureen said, looking surprised.

Danny backed toward the doorway. "I can't. Nice to meet you, Donna. See you later."

Maureen, her hair floating lightly around her head like a dark aureole, followed her to the front door. "Why do you suddenly have to leave?"

"It'll give you two a chance to talk, and I really do have a lot to do." She gave Maureen a quick hug and another kiss and went outside. The sunny, cold day made her feel as if she might crack.

Charlie was reading the Saturday morning paper at the kitchen table in a splash of sun. Tipsy, perhaps recognizing the sound of Danny, only raised his head from the same splotch of bright light.

Danny shut the cold out. "Tracy still in bed? Must have been a late night for her."

"Actually, she came home rather early. By ten-thirty."

"I was bored. I have more fun with Kim," Tracy said, padding into the kitchen on bare feet.

"He looked like a nice kid," Danny said.

"That's just it. He's such a kid. I think I need someone more mature."

Danny turned her back to hide a smile.

"What makes him such a kid?" Charlie asked, peering around the newspaper at her granddaughter.

"The only pronoun he knows is I."

"That's not being such a kid, that's being male," Charlie remarked.

"That's boring. I got in about two words." Tracy poked her head in the refrigerator.

"What say I make some pancakes?" Danny offered.

Charlie said, "Before I forget, Kara called last night."

Danny hadn't seen or talked to Kara since Tuesday. She would call her after breakfast.

She smiled at the sound of Kara's voice. "What's up?"

"Can I see you tomorrow? Peter and I are going to Florida Monday for a week."

"Why are you all of a sudden going to Florida?"

"Tell you tomorrow. I've got a showing now. Love you."

Danny started a fire in the fireplace to take the chill out of the day. Outside, a gray sky spat snow and trees bent before a wind that blew lingering, shriveled leaves across the yard. She squatted on her heels and watched the flames take hold, burning Friday's newspaper and flickering until the kindling caught fire and ignited the split oak.

Charlie relaxed on the davenport with an unopened paperback in her lap. "You remember what you said about me not bringing any men home?"

Danny nodded, recalling the words with shame.

"I just hate the thought of you growing old alone. But maybe you don't want to spend the rest of your life with some man," she added with an impish smile. "Sometimes I forget you have to decide what you want for yourself."

Danny almost admitted that she wanted to grow old with a woman, but asked instead, "You're lonely, Mom?" She sat on the hearth, her legs crossed.

"Sometimes. There are some nice things about being alone. You don't have to answer to anyone."

Feeling badly for Charlie, she briefly wondered if she herself would join the ranks of the lonely once she moved to the house she planned to build, once Tracy was gone. She asked, "Did you want to marry again, Mom?"

"Not now. I've been alone too long, too set in my ways."

Danny hadn't thought of her mother as a sexual person since she had come home one night as a teenager and heard the double bed creaking behind her parents' bedroom door. Now she wondered if her mother missed that part of a relationship.

Charlie startled her by saying, "I'm going to Buddy's for Christmas. He sent me airline tickets. I've never been out there."

"Then you should go."

"Would you and Tracy like to go with me?"

"No, Mom, you go and have a good time. We'll be just fine." She marveled at how quickly change set in. Donna showed up to see Maureen; Buddy contacted Charlie; Kara left for Florida. Maybe Maureen and Chris would come for Christmas dinner, which reminded her to call Chris about the evening.

Danny followed Maureen to the kitchen and asked innocently, "Did you have a nice day?"

Maureen gave her an appraising glance and looked away. "Yes. We had a lot of catching up to do."

Back in the living room, Danny joined in Chris and Donna's conversation. When Maureen settled on the couch next to her, Danny began to feel an almost palpable tension. The atmosphere became charged with it. All at once and with a sickening certainty, she knew that Maureen and Donna had spent some of the day in bed together.

Unwillingly, she envisioned them making love in the same bed in which she had made love to Maureen last night. Having been intimate with Maureen, she knew how Maureen would be sexual with Donna. It infuriated her. She wanted to leap to her feet and run from the apartment, from the pain. At the same time she didn't want to leave them alone so that they could do it again.

She felt eyes on her. "Did I miss something?"

"Donna's going to be teaching at the Tech too," Maureen said.

"Really? What do you teach?" Danny asked, glaring balefully at Maureen for dispensing this news. She didn't care what Donna taught. At the moment she only wanted to punch her beautiful face.

"Math."

"Her classroom is next to Michael's computer lab." Danny jumped to her feet. "Excuse me. Could I see you for a minute, Maureen?" She started blindly for the bathroom. She felt like she might puke. In the bathroom she scooped cold water from under the faucet and splashed it on her face.

Maureen closed the door and leaned against it. "What is the matter?"

"You know what the matter is," she said, water dripping off her face into the sink. The vehemence in her tone startled her. "You fucked her today, didn't you?"

"I hate that word."

"Don't avoid the question."

"Danny, don't. Can't we just have a pleasant evening?"

"With you two smirking at each other over me."

"We're not," Maureen protested. "Keep your voice down, will you?"

"Why? So we can all pretend what happened didn't happen?" Danny straightened and wiped her face angrily with the hand towel.

Maureen looked at her feet and whispered, "It wasn't planned. I care very much for you, Danny, but I love her."

"Great, terrific. I'm leaving."

"Don't, Danny. We all have to work together."

Danny started to push past her. "That'll be fun, won't it?"

Maureen grabbed her arm and Danny nearly melted into her, wanting as she did to grab back. She glanced into the black eyes, hesitated, then pulled her fury and shame back around her and slammed out of the room.

"I have to leave, Chris." She said these words as she pulled on the jacket she had jerked out of the hall closet. She knew her face was fiery red, that if she said any more she would embarrass herself by crying.

Chris apologized to Maureen as she followed Danny out the door.

Outside, Danny threw back her head and breathed in the cold. She felt she had to put distance between herself and the apartment. Opening her car door, she remembered Chris hobbling behind her. "Where do you want to go?"

"Let's go to my apartment and order pizza."

Danny nodded, letting Chris decide. She felt she was leaving behind forever something she cherished. She had experienced this pain with Rachel — the physical, gut-wrenching, nauseating pain of rejected love. She never wanted to feel it again.

Chris unlocked the door to her apartment, and the heat rushed out to meet them. Only then did she ask Danny, "What the hell was that all about? Why did you run away from there like that?"

Danny cleared her throat and tried to speak. "I can't talk about it." She paced the room, unable to sit.

Chris watched her. "Sit down and tell me."

Danny looked at Chris and saw Maureen with Donna. "I'm never going to let myself get so involved again."

"She loves this Donna?"

"Yes." Staring at her hands, Danny remembered the feel of Maureen. She began to cry and angrily wiped the tears away.

"Hey, it's okay. It really is." Chris brought her a box of tissues.

"I've got to go, Chris. I'm sorry."

Sunday afternoon, Kara brought the cool air into the house on her jeans and sweater. Her cheeks were a hot pink, her eyes a deep blue, her hair brown crinkles. Charlie had already left for the IGA; Tracy had just gone with Kim. Only Danny and Tipsy remained home.

Kara stared at Danny's still tear-swollen face and said, "What happened, darling? You look like shit."

"Thanks. Just what I wanted to hear."

"What is it?" Kara coaxed, running a gentle hand over Danny's auburn curls.

"Maureen's ex-lover returned, and they're doing it."

"Are you sure?" Danny nodded. "What's she like?"

"Gorgeous."

"I'm sorry. I know you'll find that hard to believe, but I hate seeing you hurt. I'd like to give them both a piece of my mind."

"We weren't going anywhere together anyway," Danny said listlessly. "Now why are you suddenly going to Florida?"

"Peter thinks we need a vacation. We'll see my mother while we're there and I do need to do that."

"Have you seen your counselor alone?"

"Yes."

Her interest sparking, Danny asked, "Did you tell her about us?"

"I told her that I was involved with a woman and how I felt about it, that I thought I was a lesbian. It felt good, talking about it."

All week Danny avoided the cafeteria, Maureen's hallway, Michael's area, wanting to see neither Maureen nor Donna. Michael came looking for her Wednesday evening and found her eating a sandwich in her classroom.

"You can't hide forever, sweetie."

She smiled bleakly at him. "You've met her?"

"Donna? Yes." He stood looking down at her from his considerable height, his homely features set in a compassionate frown.

"You warned me, didn't you?" She gave him a rueful smile.

"I was trying to save you some grief, not give you any. I didn't think this would happen."

"I didn't either."

"Why don't you come have a cup of coffee with me?"

"Not tonight. Ask me again a few weeks from now."

"Stop over at the house this weekend," he suggested.

"Perhaps I will."

He left her to face her class which had started straggling into the room.

The week passed in a haze of busyness, and she dreaded the weekend without Maureen, without Kara. Saturday Danny grasped at Michael's invitation and visited the house on Grove Street.

Michael met her at the door. "You know, you haven't been here since the thank you dinner."

She stepped into the foyer. "I've been so busy."

"Do you remember Neville and Robert?" He gestured toward the two men in the library. "They were at the dinner party."

She would never have recognized them, she realized with a jolt. They had lost weight and hair and carried the marks of Kaposi's sarcoma. She smiled at them, embarrassed by her own good health.

"Come on in the kitchen and talk to me. I'm making chili. Gonna blow us all into space."

Offering to help, she followed him into the huge kitchen. He made her feel useful by putting her to work chopping vegetables, while he stirred a steaming pan full of tomatoes and beans at the stove.

"Are you glad you started all this?" she asked.

"Yeah, I am. How are you doing?"

"I got through the week. Next week Kara will be back."

"Chris should be over soon. She offered to help with supper."

"Good. I need to apologize to her for last weekend."

Snow fell Thanksgiving day, at times so thick it resembled a moving white wall. The kitchen window steamed over as food cooked on the stove and in the oven. A fire burned in the fireplace. National Public

Radio filled the downstairs rooms with Beethoven's *Ninth Symphony.*

Danny had asked Chris to spend the day with them, but she was gone to her parents' farm. Danny assumed Maureen was cozily ensconced with Donna, and she felt a sharp stab of envy. How nice to be in bed with someone you loved this morning. Kara had invited Danny and her family for dinner, but Danny had declined. Under the circumstances she would have felt uncomfortable accepting Peter's hospitality.

The snow caught them by surprise. A covering had been expected, not this major storm which had built up overnight while heading their way and already dumped half of the newly predicted eight inches.

Tracy joined her mother and grandmother. Sitting cross-legged in front of the fire, she said, "Isn't this great? The snow, the food, the fire."

Danny smiled a little. It did resemble a Hallmark commercial. And this was the last holiday they would spend together this year. Not only was Charlie going to visit Buddy over Christmas, Tracy's father had asked her to spend that holiday with him.

The phone rang and Tracy got to her feet to answer it. Danny could hear her voice but not her words. She sounded upset, angry, and slammed the receiver into its cradle.

"Something wrong?" Danny asked, watching her daughter return to her spot by the fire.

Tracy put an arm around the dog, who curled up against her. "I hate Scott. I won't go out with him and he's saying all kinds of stuff about me."

"Like what?" Charlie asked.

Tracy's eyes met and held Danny's. "He told Kim Mom was queer and I was too, and that's why I wouldn't date him."

For the space of a second, Danny thought her heart stopped. Then it pumped blood through her body so rapidly that she broke out in sweat and her breathing quickened. She could not take her gaze from her daughter's, even though she knew the crimson flush gave her away. She licked her lips.

"Mom?" Tracy said questioningly. "I didn't believe him, Mom."

Danny knew she was asking her to refute the accusation, but she couldn't speak.

"Well, if that isn't the most ridiculous thing I ever heard," Charlie huffed and then looked at her daughter.

The silence that followed fed Danny's panic. She heard the fire, her own breathing, the hissing of snow outside the windows. Deny it, she told herself. They want to hear that it's not true. But every time she opened her mouth to say something, she made no sound. Pulling her eyes away from Tracy's, she turned toward her mother and realized that Charlie had just needed to hear someone say the words to know they were true. Somehow she had to get through this day, she thought, going to the kitchen.

Tracy was right behind her. She leaned on the counter, trying to look into her mother's averted face. "Mom? Is that why you left Dad?"

Danny breathed a lengthy sigh. Nothing was ever that simple. "No, Tracy."

"But it's true then? You're queer? You do that with women?"

Danny flinched at being called queer by her daughter; she hated the word.

"I shouldn't have been born," the girl said. "You couldn't have wanted me."

"I did want you. Why do you say that?" Danny asked unable to follow Tracy's logic.

"You didn't want Dad."

"Oh, that's not true. I told you I loved your dad and I love you."

"Your marriage was a lie."

"Stop it," Danny said sharply. Her voice and hands shook. "Stop telling me how it was. I lived it. It wasn't a lie. You weren't a mistake. Making you was the best thing I ever did. Your dad and I just didn't last."

"Because you wanted a woman."

The accusation stung because it was at least partially true. And she couldn't tell Tracy that her father had betrayed the marriage, too. It seemed unfair to have to stand accused and not parcel out the blame as it should be shared. "There's never just one reason and one person at fault."

"You're sick, Mom." The girl turned and fled the room, brushing past Charlie who stood in the doorway.

Danny felt drained and shaken. "Well, Mom?" she said, facing her own mother.

"Have you looked at the food? The water's boiling away on those sweet potatoes."

Danny laughed shakily, relieved that Charlie chose not to confront her. She wondered if they would eat today, if she'd be able to pry Tracy out of her room. Emptying the pan of water, she set the potatoes to cool.

When she returned to the living room, nothing had changed. Tracy wasn't there, but Tipsy still lay curled by the fire. The snow fell furiously outside the windows. The furniture hadn't moved. Yet their lives were different. Relationships had shifted and would have to be adjusted. She had forced change into their lives by acknowledging with silence the innuendo regarding her sex life. She stretched out on the recliner and closed her eyes, listening to the choral part of the *Ninth Symphony*.

She wondered how Kara's day was going, if Chris was enjoying Thanksgiving on the farm, if Maureen and Donna were out of bed yet, how many guests Michael and Tony would feed today.

At three in the afternoon with dinner preparations completed, Danny knocked on her daughter's bedroom door. "Come on down, honey. There's good food on the table."

"I'm not hungry," Tracy said. "Go away. You ruined my life."

Danny smiled humorlessly at the histrionics, the myopic immediacy of youth. "I can't ruin your life, Tracy. Only you can do that."

"I wish I'd never been born." Tracy's voice rose to a wail. "I can't go back to school and face everybody."

"Why not? You don't have to make a general announcement."

"I have to lie to everybody, even Kim."

"You don't have to lie to anyone. It's nobody's business."

"Leave me alone." Tracy sounded desolate.

Danny longed to hold her, to let her know that the world as she knew it had not ended, but she decided it was better if she didn't push. She turned and went downstairs where Charlie waited on the couch, staring out the window at the falling snow, at the day already turning into night.

Danny anticipated a walk in the snow after dinner, something to look forward to. "She won't come down. Want to go ahead and eat?"

"May as well. The food's getting cold."

Halfway through the meal, Tracy appeared. She pulled out a chair and sat down, her heart-shaped face puffy from crying. Silently, she heaped food on her plate and tasted it.

Danny glanced at Charlie and they exchanged a slight smile. Danny wondered what thoughts her mother harbored because, unlike Tracy, Charlie had said nothing about the morning's revelations.

After dinner, Danny put on a hooded sweatshirt and heavy jacket. "Anyone want to go for a walk?"

"I'm going to Kim's," Tracy announced sullenly, her chin jutting defiantly.

Danny studied her. Maybe she needed a little distance. At least she would know where Tracy was. "You can't drive, you know, and it's a long walk."

"I don't care." Tracy shoved her arms into her winter jacket and donned heavy boots. "I'm spending the night there."

Danny ached for her, hated letting her go away even for a night with this estrangement between them. "I'll walk you there."

"If you get stranded, give me a call," Charlie said.

Stepping outside into a white, muffled world, Danny paused to look. Snow still fell in the windless night, but the leading edge of the storm had passed through and the flakes had diminished in size and number. Eight inches on the ground, even with no drifts, made walking difficult. A plow with yellow lights flashing surged along Elm Street, piling snow high along the curbs and driveways.

Danny, who had always loved the snow, gazed with wonder at the hushed, alabaster world, while Tipsy floundered in its depths and urinated hot, yellow holes into its purity. "Beautiful, isn't it?"

Leaning forward against the weight of her backpack, Tracy grunted without lifting her face.

Another curve had been thrown into her daughter's life, Danny reflected with a glance at her offspring. The girl had managed the hurdle of her parents' divorce, the move to Edgemont, all the while, no doubt, struggling to understand her own identity. Danny realized she had to help her daughter cope with this mental muddying of her mother's image. "What are you thinking, sweetie?"

Hands thrust deep in her pockets, Tracy kicked at a pile of snow along the curb. "You lied to me."

"Think about it, honey. It's not something one announces publicly."

"I'm not the public. Are you ashamed?"

Danny gave some thought to the question before answering. "No. I had nothing to do with my sexual orientation."

"You're saying you're not to blame for your actions?"

"I'm saying I'm not responsible for my feelings."

Tracy snorted. "You're still responsible for what you do with your feelings."

"That's true."

"You don't have to sleep with women."

180

Danny pulled Tipsy out of a snow bank. "Why shouldn't I be able to express my love for someone?"

"Love," Tracy mocked. "You call that love?"

"Yes, I do. One loves a woman much like a man. It's not so different."

"I don't want to talk about it."

"Well, when you do, come to me."

They walked the rest of the way to Kim's house in silence.

Charlie had left the light over the kitchen sink on for her. The fire in the fireplace burned low in the quiet house, the flames rising and falling like heartbeats.

XII

Tracy stayed away Friday and Saturday, calling to say that she would not be home but that she was okay. Danny got her skis out and took to the freshly groomed trails, striding out alone Friday and with Kara on Saturday. The chill beauty of fresh snow, hiding the drabness of winter, soothed her. Exercise eased her frustration.

She confided the Thanksgiving Day fiasco to a horrified Kara while they pulled their boots on in the steamy warming lodge. "I'm scared for Tracy,

Kara. I'm afraid she'll do something stupid to get even with me, something that will hurt her."

Kara sighed loudly. "I know. Every time the kids get really angry, I worry that they'll do something crazy. The strangest thoughts go through their heads."

Danny wanted reassurance, not confirmation of her fears for Tracy. She grunted as she tugged at her shoelaces, tightening them. She stood up and stretched. "Ready?"

The day was dying when Danny dropped Kara off at her home and drove to her own. It went hurriedly now, the sun dropping to the horizon, leaving behind a pale mauve sky that faded quickly into night.

Except for Tipsy, the house was empty. She ate alone with the dog near her feet. As she finished a plate of leftovers, the back door opened and Tracy staggered through it.

The girl made an attempt to straighten when she saw Danny at the kitchen table.

Dismayed, Danny said, "Oh, Tracy," over the ringing phone.

Kim's mother told her that the two girls had emptied at least one bottle of vodka, that her husband had driven Tracy home. When Danny hung up, Tracy was gone from sight.

She found her daughter retching in the upstairs bathroom. Talking to Tracy in her present condition seemed pointless. She helped her to bed, deciding she would speak to her in the morning.

The next day the girl, looking miserable, lay curled like a shrimp in her sour-smelling bedroom. She peered at her mother out of red-streaked eyes. "I suppose you never got smashed at my age?"

Danny took a deep breath. "Of course I did, but not at a friend's house on her parents' liquor."

Tracy looked away. "I didn't do it alone."

"Kim's mother thinks you two should be apart for a while."

"I don't care. I don't care about anything."

Thanksgiving vacation dragged toward a welcome end, and time picked up speed. The following work week passed quickly for Danny. Charlie still made no mention of what Danny mentally referred to as the Thanksgiving bombshell. Tracy slunk around the house, once again uncommunicative and sullen.

On Wednesday Neville suffered a seizure and died, reminding those who mourned him of their own tenuous mortality. Neville's death loosed the cat from the bag and the neighborhood rose in complaint, claiming Michael and Tony had lied about the purpose of their house. It was not really a bed and breakfast; it was a home for AIDS patients and therefore needed a different license.

Michael and Tony countered by professing they did not discriminate among their guests, that anyone was welcome, including those with illnesses.

Shaken by Neville's death and the resulting controversy, Danny came home from the house on Grove Street Friday night to find Charlie frantic.

"Why don't you ever tell me where you are?" Ashen-faced, Charlie handed Danny a crumpled piece of paper.

Danny read it with a frown. *I'm going to live with Dad.* She raised her gaze, seeing her own worry and fear mirrored in her mother's eyes. It was dark outside and Roselawn was two hundred miles away. "When did you find this? Where?" She gestured with the brief message.

"In her room. I thought maybe she was asleep, because I hadn't seen or heard her. She usually leaves notes on the kitchen table when she's going somewhere. And she hadn't called." Charlie's voice trailed off.

"How would she get there?" Danny asked herself, as much as her mother. Hitchhike? Would she be so foolish? In her anger, maybe. She reached for the phone, then had to look up Craig's new number.

"Maybe you should call Kim first," Charlie suggested.

She squeezed her mother's hand, feeling skin soft and dry, and looked up the number. "Kim, do you have any idea where Tracy is?" she asked, giving Kim a chance to level with her. She'd get more out of her that way. When Kim hesitated, she added, "She left a note that she was going to live with her dad."

"I know," Kim said, sounding young and vulnerable.

Danny thought of her daughter, alone in the night. She wanted to cry. "How was she going to get there?"

Kim cleared her throat. "I took her to the bus station. She's okay, Mrs. J." It was what Kim called Danny. "I saw her get on."

"Thanks, Kim." She hung up and smiled tremulously at Charlie. "She took the bus." Then she punched in Craig's number.

The phone rang four times before the answer machine kicked in. She listened to a strange woman's voice ask her to leave a message. She left her name and number, requesting that Craig give her a call. Slowly cradling the receiver, she chewed on the inside of her mouth.

"Maybe he went to pick her up," Charlie said, breaking into her thoughts.

"A woman taped the message. He's living with someone."

"Do you think you got the wrong number?"

Danny shook her head. "She said that she and Craig were sorry they had missed the call."

Charlie said, "Tracy won't like that, will she?"

Danny grinned wryly and shook her head. "No, she sure won't."

When the phone rang an hour later, Danny jumped for it.

"She's all right. She's here," Craig said. "I can't get her to tell me what happened, though. You want to tell me?"

Weak with relief and feeling exhausted, Danny replied, "No, let her tell you. I don't suppose she wants to talk to me."

"Just a minute." She heard muffled voices, then he said, "Not right now she doesn't. I'll call you in a couple days. Okay?"

She and Charlie went to bed. Danny slept late Saturday morning and woke up feeling sluggish and depressed. Padding around the house in socks and sweats with Tipsy dogging her, she was unable to settle anywhere. Kara was coming over that afternoon. She called her as soon as Charlie left for the IGA and asked if she could come earlier.

"You didn't sound so good." Her face ruddy, her hair windblown, Kara swept the cold in with her. "You don't look so good, either."

Still sluffing around aimlessly, Danny grinned. Kara would always make an impressive entrance, she thought. "Thanks," she said dryly. Slumped at the kitchen table, she told her about Tracy.

Kara's expressive face registered dismay. "Aw, sweetie." She got up and took Danny in her arms. "Come on. Let's go somewhere more comfortable."

"I don't want to go to bed."

"I was thinking of the couch, Danny. Sex is the furthest thing from my mind right now," Kara assured her.

Danny curled up against her. "He's living with some woman."

Kissing Danny's forehead, Kara said, "Craig? If that's the case, don't bother to change the sheets on Tracy's bed. She'll be back tomorrow."

Danny thought of this while waiting for Tracy at the bus station the following Saturday. It hadn't been a good week. She had run into Maureen in the hallway at the Tech. Shifting her feet uncomfortably, she recalled the meeting. Maureen had forced a confrontation, stopping to speak to her. She had looked wonderful. Danny attributed the inner glow to her renewed romance with Donna.

Smiling tentatively, her black eyes alight, she had said, "I miss you, Danny."

Danny had been unable to think of an answer to this. "You look happy."

"I am. Can we be friends?" Maureen had searched her eyes.

Shaking her head, Danny had replied, "Not yet."

Nodding, Maureen had smiled a little sadly. "Keep in touch. Say hello to Kara."

The bus hissed to a stop and she watched the passengers descend, stepping out into the brisk December day. Diesel fumes burned her nose and eyes. Her heart twisted when Tracy got off. Standing next to the bus, an overnight bag in one hand, Tracy brushed the hair away from her face with the other. Her jeans looked a little baggy in the knees and she wore a sweatshirt under her jacket. Danny knew immediately that the girl had returned under duress.

She hugged her daughter, feeling the taut muscles and delicate bones that made up her structure. "Good to have you home, honey."

Tracy grunted and backed off. She threw her bag into the Escort.

"That your only suitcase?" No wonder she looked a little seedy. Had she planned to send for her clothes? There were no answers. Tracy wasn't talking.

Without any spirit for the season, Danny shopped for Christmas. Using the money Craig had given her as a Christmas gift, Tracy had purchased an airline ticket. She was now going to California with her grandmother. Before Charlie and Tracy left for the holiday the three of them exchanged gifts.

Attempting to put a good face on their early

celebration, Charlie and Danny prepared a sumptuous meal. A small Christmas tree cut from a nearby tree farm glowed with lights in a corner of the living room. Disheartened by their dismal efforts at conversation during dinner, Danny expected nothing from the remainder of the evening. She felt their attempts to celebrate only emphasized their estrangement and she wanted to cry.

Having taken great care to find suitable gifts, she watched first Tracy and then Charlie open their presents. She had bought Tracy a boom box complete with radio, tape deck and compact disc player, and she smiled at the expression of pleased surprise on her daughter's face. For Charlie she had chosen a gift certificate to be used to replace the ancient davenport of Danny's childhood.

Then Danny opened Charlie's present and stared at it as it lay in her lap. Charlie could not afford expensive presents, she knew. What rested in her hands was a small bronze statue of a nude woman, curled forward as if in thought, seated with hands clasped around one bent leg. Danny stared at it, thinking it exquisite, wondering where Charlie had found it and, more to the point, what the gift meant. Looking somewhat bewildered, she met her mother's eyes.

Charlie laughed a little in apparent embarrassment. "You don't like it? I thought you would."

"I love it," Danny replied, close to tears. "Thanks, Mom." She continued to stare at Charlie for a few moments more. "It's beautiful." Was this Charlie's way of accepting her?

Tracy looked indifferent as Danny picked up her

gift. She had even less money to spend than Charlie, of course, and Danny carefully removed the tape from the small package.

"You can rip the paper, Mom," she said impatiently, sounding more like her old self.

Inside was a framed eight-by-ten print, a photograph of herself and Tracy taken by Charlie last summer. Sun-browned and windblown they laughed at the camera, each with an arm around the other. She had never seen it but she recalled the time and setting. "We were at the lake. Remember?" Tracy said grudgingly. "I had it made in September."

"I remember. It's very good of both of us. I guess we do look alike." Smiling with pleasure, she admired the picture. She would cherish it, would hang it in her room where she could see it before sleep and after waking. "Thank you, Tracy. Thank you both. I love my gifts." And she did.

Danny spent Christmas at Michael and Tony's. She had told Charlie and Tracy not to worry, that she wouldn't be alone for the holiday, and had heard Tracy mutter, "Who's worried?" But she felt a little lonesome at the big table with only close acquaintances for companions.

Both Chris and Kara had invited her to their homes for the day, and she had declined. Kara had been at Danny's house yesterday, had spent a few hours in Danny's bed, locked with her in passionate embrace.

There were seven of them at the table: Michael and Tony and Danny, Kevin and Mark, Robert and another guest, both with full-blown AIDS. Robert sat next to Danny. She supposed he would be next to die, but he exuded cheer.

"Want me to offer up a prayer?" he asked.

Michael looked mildly alarmed. Not a religious man, he had once confided his healthy fear of organized religion to Danny.

Robert closed his eyes and lifted his wasted face toward the chandelier. "Neville, you devil, are you there?"

Chills raced up Danny's spine until she sneaked a look at his face and saw his sad smile.

"Give us a sign. Flicker the lights or something. I miss you, you damn pagan. Merry Christmas."

"We all miss you, Neville," Tony added. "Amen."

"Does it seem a little strange, sweetie, to be having Christmas dinner with a bunch of queens?" Michael asked as he carved the turkey.

"It feels good," Danny lied, feeling misplaced.

Robert patted her leg. "This is the best Christmas I ever had. Good friends, good food, good drink, good care."

The disclosure depressed Danny. Surely he must have had Christmases when he had enjoyed better health and a hopeful future. She knew he was only thirty-two.

She had seen Maureen and Donna yesterday. That caused some of the distress she now felt. They had been in the IGA. Taking a deep breath, she had wished them a happy holiday. Then she had immediately checked out without finishing her shopping. Would she spend the next months fleeing every time she saw them?

The evening at Michael and Tony's ended in the sunroom, where they ate dessert and listened to music and talked quietly. She went home around ten, driving through empty, white streets.

On New Year's Eve, Chris and Danny went to the only gay bar in town — a smoke-filled barn of a place, so dark inside that it was nearly impossible to identify anyone more than a few feet away.

The beat of music resounded off the ceiling and walls, and one song ran into another. Strobe lights shot lines of color through smoke. Huge video screens flashed writhing, mouthing images. The only one she recognized was Madonna.

Danny and Chris danced, their movements disjointed and unreal in the jabbing lights. Out of necessity conversations became shouting matches, so they talked little. They welcomed in the New Year singing "Auld Lang Syne," swaying in unison with the others on the dance floor. The many voices, filling the building, sent shivers through Danny.

XIII

Danny chose for her lot a log house design, and construction started as soon as the weather permitted. As a mother might watch her child grow, she watched the basement dug, its walls and floor poured, the subflooring and studs and joists go up, the roof covered, the logs laid, the windows fitted, the plumbing and heating installed, the finger system and well dug. When the inside became ready for finish work, she planned to do it. And she had plenty of helpers waiting in the wings — Kara, Chris, Michael, Tony, Tracy, even Charlie.

In mid-June, when the bathroom was finished, she moved in. The carpenters continued to hammer and drill around her, but she could wait no longer. Tracy stayed on with her grandma, promising to join her mother as soon as she could be assured of not being wakened early in the morning by workmen. Her anger toward Danny had relented into a wary acceptance, which seemed to hinge on avoiding any reference to Danny's sexual orientation. A game of Let's Pretend, Danny had told Kara.

The first Tuesday night Kara came by with a picnic dinner of potato salad, cole slaw and cold turkey ham. She also brought iced champagne, a tablecloth, and two candles with holders. They set a plywood plank on a couple of sawhorses and sat on lawn chairs in the dining area.

Dismay at the makeshift arrangement leaked into Kara's voice. "Darling, you must get some furniture."

"I know. You can help me pick it out. But right now I could care less. I only need a bed, a lamp, a chair which I already have."

"And me, I hope," Kara added. "I am so horny."

Danny laughed. "And you, of course. How's the counseling going?"

Candlelight flickered over Kara's face. "We've gone round and round. I see the counselor alone every other time. I really like her. We only go once a month, but it's about time to end it."

"What do you talk about when Peter goes?"

"Mostly, the faults we see in each other. Peter says I'm always rushing off somewhere, that I direct household activities like a female Hitler."

Danny whooped with laughter, thinking how much she enjoyed just being with Kara. "Are you and Peter going to make it?"

Kara smiled ruefully and toyed with her champagne glass. "I don't know. I want to be with you so much it's a physical ache, but I don't know if I can do that either."

"You'll know if the time comes."

Kara snuffed out the candles and drew Danny down onto a rug. The patio doors were flung open to the deck overlooking the lake. A soft breeze touched them where they lay gazing through the screen at the dark trees, the flat sheen of lake beyond, the black star-studded sky.

"It's the dark of the moon, potato planting time."

Danny snuggled closer, burying her face in Kara's breasts. She could never resist their soft fullness. She breathed in the familiar smell of Kara's cologne, the soap she used, the odor of her smooth skin, and she sighed with pleasure.

Kara ran her fingers through Danny's hair. "What do you want me to do, Danny? Should I leave him or not?"

"I can't answer that for you." Danny suckled a warm nipple, then moved to the other.

Kara rolled toward Danny and held her tightly with both arms. "Do you want me to move in with you? I need you to be honest."

"Yes," came the muffled reply. Surprised because she hadn't needed to think about it, Danny pulled herself up face to face with Kara.

Kara smiled, her teeth gleaming whitely in her shadowy features.

"But not yet," Danny modified. "I think I need to be alone for a while."

The grin vanished. "That wasn't nice, Danielle, to make me hope and take it away."

"My glands were talking. I had my face in your wonderful bosom."

"You're right, though. I need time too," Kara said, sounding troubled.

They became a tangle of limbs and mouths and hands, making love in the warm darkness. Outside, muted rustling sounds turned into crashing.

"Damn," Danny breathed into Kara's mouth. "It's probably Dupris and his dogs."

"Maybe we should go to the bedroom," Kara whispered, her body gone rigid in Danny's arms.

"Okay." Danny got to her hands and knees and crawled down the hall. She heard Kara dragging something with her, probably their clothes. Pausing in mid-crawl, she turned back to Kara, who bumped into her and let out a small cry of alarm. "Kara, give me my shorts and shirt. I've got to at least make sure that the screens are locked."

The nightlight in the bathroom guided her down the hall to the bed where Kara waited. "That goddamn man. If I believed in guns, I'd shoot him," she said, climbing between the sheets. Then asked in momentary panic, when no one responded, "That is you, Kara, isn't it?"

"It's me, sweetie, but I'm afraid I've lost all passion."

Danny put her arms around Kara and pulled herself to her. "Change your mind about wanting to live with me?"

"Well, I must admit it seems somewhat less desirable. Aren't you scared here alone?"

"Sure, sometimes. There are all these night sounds I can't identify. I think Dupris and I have an unspoken truce, though. I make no attempt to keep him off my land and he leaves me alone."

"What do you mean he leaves you alone? What on earth do you think he'd do to you?"

"Who knows?" The bedroom was so black that Danny couldn't see Kara, could only hear her voice. Once, when the lights went out during a storm, she had tried to eat in nearly total darkness and had been unable to fork the food off her plate or get it to her mouth. This reminded her of that time and she found it just as difficult to make love in such blackness. "I've got to turn on a light."

Kara froze in Danny's arms, physically restraining her. "No. Don't move. Let's just go to sleep."

Tracy moved into her mother's new house, and Charlie turned up as often as anyone. Weekends became long parties. Friends came and went with such frequency that Danny no longer made a special effort to greet them or tell them goodbye. They nearly always brought food and helped with whatever needed doing, which assured their welcome. There was usually someone with whom to talk, to eat, to fritter away time.

Danny began to long for a little privacy. She resented having to meet Kara at the Budget Inn again. She had enjoyed their brief time together at the lake, making love in her own place. She no longer wanted to go to even minor lengths to hide Kara, but hide they must.

Therefore, it came as a mixed bag of worry and relief when Kara gave her the news that Peter knew about the two of them. Kara's face flushed with the heat of discussing their exposure. "He's been following us. I couldn't even look at him," she said glumly.

Kara had found Danny casting a fishing line from the short pier Michael and Tony had helped her put in. The sun slid toward the horizon, a huge red orb. And as Kara spoke, a bass hit Danny's jitterbug, forcing her to concentrate on landing the fish. In its struggle to escape the bass leaped twisting from the water and fell back with a splash. "Look at it," Danny said excitedly. "It's immense."

"I see it," Kara said with obvious irritation. "This is important, Danielle."

"I know. Just let me get this baby in and we'll talk." But when Danny reeled the fish close enough to net it, the bass shook free of the lure. "Damn. I would've let it go. I just wanted to measure it. What do you think? Twenty inches?"

Kara snapped, "I don't know and I don't give a shit."

"That's unpleasant of you," Danny remarked,

bringing in the rest of her line and setting the pole on the pier. She lowered herself onto the wood surface and patted the space next to her. "Sit."

Kara sat, removed her shoes, and put her feet in the water beside Danny's.

"Tell me now and don't leave out anything."

Kara simply said, "He knows."

"Look at those colors," Danny exclaimed, gazing at the muted shades of red across sky and lake.

"I see," Kara murmured and sighed deeply.

"So, now what? Do you move in with me or what?"

"He preempted me. He moved out. Damn." Kara slugged the pier in an uncharacteristic display of anger. "I knew I should have left first."

"Does that mean you have to stay there?"

"Somebody has to. The kids are unhappy. Johnny mopes around like he's lost his best friend. Laura's angry with me, blames me for her father leaving. I suppose I am to blame, though." She sat silent for a moment, then continued, "I'm going to suggest putting the house on the market. I can't afford it. But that'll upset the kids even more." She stirred the water with her feet and sighed again. "It's all so goddamned complicated, Danny."

"It always is. It's easier just to stay put. No muss, no fuss."

Kara gave her a sidelong look and a little smile. "I wanted him to do this and here I am complaining about it. I didn't want to make the first move."

Danny lay back on the pier, propped her head up with her hands. A warm breeze brushed softly over her. The colors in the sky paled to pinkish gray before her eyes and then dimmed to gentle darkness. A sliver of new moon rode low in the west. Danny spoke softly. "I love it here."

"Winter might change your perspective," Kara remarked. "The drive to the Tech on icy roads through mountains of snow, cabin fever when you can't readily escape, lonesome solitude without family, friends or neighbors within easy reach, short days and long cold nights."

"Thanks for pointing that out to me."

Sensing another presence, they peered toward shore in the near dark.

"Just me and Kim," Tracy called. "Kim's staying over. That okay, Mom?"

"Sure." And then quietly to Kara, "I wish you could stay over."

"So do I, sweetie. But the kids'll be expecting me. Ain't motherhood great? We get most of the blame and most of the work and have to share the glory with papa. If that isn't a pisser."

The warm night surrounded them. Insects chirped and chirred, a few lightning bugs flickered along the shore, an occasional frog chunked.

Kara got up and brushed her shorts off. "I have to go home. Johnny is so needy right now."

"What about Tuesday?"

Kara shrugged, showed white teeth in the darkness. "The day doesn't matter now."

"In three weeks Tracy will be gone to school and we can do whatever we want here." Tracy and Kim had both been accepted at the University of Wisconsin, Madison. They had applied to other schools, but only as back-ups. Neither wanted to go anywhere else.

"I never thought I'd say this to you, but right now desire is the last thing on my mind."

Danny rented a U-Haul trailer to pack Tracy and Kim's belongings in and drove the two of them to the university in Madison. She knew she should feel more abandoned than she did when she kissed Tracy and waved goodbye to her. She felt an almost embarrassing sense of freedom when she pulled out into the flow of parental traffic heading home, as she watched Tracy shrink in the rearview mirror.

Helping her daughter pack last night, she had made one last attempt to talk about their estrangement. "Have you thought about getting counseling, sweetie?"

Tracy had given her a bleak look. "It won't change anything, will it?"

"It won't change the way I am, but it might change your perception of it."

"I see it as it is."

She had remarked gently, "You see it as you want to."

"I don't want to talk about it." Leaning on the too-full suitcase while Danny zipped it shut, Tracy had asked gruffly, "Will your insurance cover counseling, *if* I decide to go?"

Danny had smiled and given her a hug. Since the Tech offered such good coverage, she had put Tracy on her policy. "Yes. Just let me know."

She had seen little of Kara since Peter had left home. When they had made quick, furtive love at the new house, both had worried about who might knock on the door. It had put them in a bad mood. Kara had accused Danny of willfully withdrawing, and it was true that she went less and less to town. Is this what happened to people who made the move from city to country? Those who wanted to see her had to take the time to drive to the lake.

She passed Dupris out by the road with Jimbo and Mack and enveloped them in a cloud of dust. He still roamed the surrounding woods at night, the dogs yowling at all hours, occasional gunshots rending the quiet. Last winter she had snapped the steel jaws shut on countless traps set on her newly acquired land. Mostly, though, she didn't want to know what he was doing, especially if she couldn't stop him.

As she unlocked her door, she felt lonesome for the first time that day. Walking through the empty rooms, stopping to look at the lake, she pressed her forehead against the glass patio doors. The sun glowered behind heavy clouds. Between dark trees, gloomy in the dour day, she glimpsed the water — gunmetal gray and restive in the late afternoon.

She called her mother. "I'm back."

"It went all right then," Charlie said. "I thought you might stop by. I even fixed extra food."

"I'm sorry, Mom. I didn't think to stop, I was so glad to be home again."

Then she called Kara. "Can you get away?" She heard Kara sigh and thought how frequently Kara sighed these days.

"I'm supposed to drop everything and come running?" Kara snapped. "Why didn't you ask me earlier?"

"Don't give me a hard time. I'm tired and lonesome."

Kara's voice softened. "I can't, Danny. Peter's coming over tonight. We're going to talk divorce. You know, who gets what. I'm crabby because I want to be with you, because I would be if you had any foresight."

When Danny hung up, night had settled over the woods and was closing in on the lake. Knowing Chris was most likely with Tina, she nevertheless dialed her number and listened to her answer machine.

She would have walked down to the lake, but being alone in the dark sometimes frightened her. She scared herself, imagining danger lurking in the shadows in the form of a bear or rapist or something equally formidable and unlikely.

Sitting in the sagging armchair with the good reading lamp hanging over it, she picked up the book she had started a week ago. She read the same paragraph at least three times before putting it down and going to the refrigerator to search for food. After eating leftovers, she returned to the chair and switched off the light. Stretching out, she listened to the music of the night — tried to separate the sounds into categories and the categories into individual noises.

Finally, because she could think of nothing else she wanted to do, she took herself to bed. Disgusted with her inability to concentrate and now unable to sleep, she tossed until exhaustion permitted her a fitful dozing.

* * * * *

As Danny drove home through the piles of snow Kara had predicted with such accuracy last summer, she thought of her conversation with Michael that afternoon. He had asked her if she was lonely, if she wanted to move back to town during the winter months. He had told her that things were working out well at the bed and breakfast, that she could stay with them. She had said thanks but no thanks.

The Escort skidded sideways, and Danny lifted her foot off the accelerator until it straightened. She admitted to herself that there were nights when the howling of wind through the pines caused a lonesome ache inside her, when cold rain lashing at the windows made her feel trapped. She had looked forward to being snowed or rained in, to building a fire against the elements and reading before the flames, but when that time inevitably arrived, she found she wanted the option of going outside.

A purplish smudge marked the horizon where the sun had set. Snowbanks gleamed whitely in her headlights. Tracy had gone back to school two weeks ago, when Christmas vacation ended, leaving the house cruelly quiet. January promised to be a long month.

The car bounced the length of the driveway, its headlights pointing out the trees on either side, rising and falling with the grade of the road. Danny's heart lifted at the sight of Kara's Grand Am parked near the garage. Warm, welcoming light spilled from the kitchen window onto the snowy backyard. How different from the feeling when the house greeted her dark and silent and cold.

As she climbed the steps to the back stoop, she heard Jimbo and Mack belling in the clear night.

Breathing icy air, she shot a glance at the sky, at stars shining out of the blackness overhead. It would be a frigid night with no cloud cover to keep the lid on the day's little heat. When she opened the back door, a great horned owl hooted and she paused for the answering call.

"Hi, sweetie." Kara turned a cheerful face toward Danny. She stood at the stove dressed in jeans, flannel shirt, and apron. "This is a spooky place without you around and with those dogs howling like wolves out there," she said with a shiver.

Realizing she had forgotten how lonely it was to come home to no one, until she came home to someone again, Danny laughed softly. "What are you doing?"

"What the hell does it look like? I'm fixing dinner. Chicken stir fry, rice, salad, rolls, wine. We're celebrating."

Danny clasped Kara from behind and buried her face in her sweet-smelling neck. "What's the occasion?"

"Your nose is like ice, lady." Kara turned and wrapped Danny in her arms, enveloping her in softness. "We accepted an offer on the house today. Now go put on something more comfortable and hurry back. But on the way make it warmer in here, will you? I refuse to live at such uncivilized temperatures."

"I had the fire all laid. Why didn't you put a match to it?" Danny asked, setting flame to paper under kindling and logs.

"I didn't know if the draft was open, and I wasn't going to stick my head up the chimney to check."

Danny changed into sweats and returned to the kitchen. Again she took hold of Kara and hugged her. "God, it's good to have you here. What can I do to help?"

"Open the wine."

"Tell me now, what's going on?" Taking a bottle of Chardonnay from the refrigerator, Danny removed the cork.

"We signed the offer to purchase. Closing is three weeks from now. I'm going to let Johnny live with his dad." Kara's voice broke on the last sentence and Danny gave her another quick hug. Kara had agonized for weeks over Johnny's wish to live with his father, had wanted to fight it.

"It's best, if that's what he wants, Kara," Danny said softly. "He'll come around quicker if you support him."

"It hurts. What if Tracy had wanted to stay with her father?"

Danny thought she would have fought it, but Tracy was her only child. "That would have put too much distance between us. Johnny won't be far. Laura's going to live with us, isn't she?"

"I don't know. She's not keen about moving out of town. She might just come on the weekends." Kara sniffed and leaned on the stove.

Realizing the extent of Kara's hurt, her sense of loss, Danny moved toward her, took her in her arms, and pulled her close. She felt Kara melting into her, heard the cry tearing from her throat.

"Oh, Kara, I'm so sorry."

"I wanted the divorce," Kara reasoned through the sobs. "This comes with it. God, it hurts to feel rejected by my own kids."

"It's like you said. They don't want to leave town where their friends are. Tracy didn't want to leave Roselawn."

Kara, her eyes awash with tears, heaved a sigh and asked, "Am I being foolish to want something different after all these years? Should I just have hung in there and not rocked the boat?"

Smiling gently, Danny shook her head. "You're brave. It takes courage to make such a change. It'll get better."

"I hope so. This whole miserable business has been like pulling teeth. There's been nothing easy about it."

"How well I know. Now what happened to the celebration?"

Mopping her eyes, Kara's smile shimmered through tears. "There are advantages in not always having the kids. They're with Peter. I can stay the night."

"When are you staying for good?" Danny asked as they sat down to dinner.

"Soon. But I was thinking that maybe we could take an apartment or perhaps I could buy a house in town for the winters. What do you think? There's this nice little place around the corner from Michael and Tony's."

"You can buy it if you want, Kara. I'd like to give living here a try first, though."

"All right, Danny. We'll do it your way. There will always be houses for sale."

Danny had no doubt their friendship would last a lifetime, but she wasn't sure that their desire for each other would. She didn't profess to understand the attraction. Perhaps because they were both passionate women, one's passion fed on the other's. And right now she felt a love for Kara that she felt for no one else. A love that grew out of liking began on solid ground, she thought. She gave a little laugh.

"What is it?" Kara asked.

"Us. Who would have guessed we'd end up together like this?"

Kara smiled. "One of the unexpected rewards of friendship."

A few of the publications of
THE NAIAD PRESS, INC.
P.O. Box 10543 • Tallahassee, Florida 32302
Phone (904) 539-5965
Toll-Free Order Number: 1-800-533-1973
Mail orders welcome. Please include 15% postage.

LONG GOODBYES by Nikki Baker. 256 pp. A Virginia Kelly
mystery. 3rd in a series. ISBN 1-56280-042-6 $9.95

FRIENDS AND LOVERS by Jackie Calhoun. 224 pp. Mid-western
Lesbian lives and loves. ISBN 1-56280-041-8 9.95

THE CAT CAME BACK by Hilary Mullins. 208 pp. Highly praised
Lesbian novel. ISBN 1-56280-040-X 9.95

BEHIND CLOSED DOORS by Robbi Sommers. 192 pp. Hot, erotic
short stories. ISBN 1-56280-039-6 9.95

CLAIRE OF THE MOON by Nicole Conn. 192 pp. See the movie —
read the book! ISBN 1-56280-038-8 10.95

SILENT HEART by Claire McNab. 192 pp. Exotic Lesbian
romance. ISBN 1-56280-036-1 9.95

HAPPY ENDINGS by Kate Brandt. 272 pp. Intimate conversations
with Lesbian authors. ISBN 1-56280-050-7 10.95

THE SPY IN QUESTION by Amanda Kyle Williams. 256 pp. 4th
spy novel featuring Lesbian agent Madison McGuire.
ISBN 1-56280-037-X 9.95

SAVING GRACE by Jennifer Fulton. 240 pp. Adventure and
romantic entanglement. ISBN 1-56280-051-5 9.95

THE YEAR SEVEN by Molleen Zanger. 208 pp. Women surviving
in a new world. ISBN 1-56280-034-5 9.95

CURIOUS WINE by Katherine V. Forrest. 176 pp. Tenth
Anniversary Edition. The most popular contemporary Lesbian
love story. ISBN 1-56280-053-1 9.95

CHAUTAUQUA by Catherine Ennis. 192 pp. Exciting, romantic
adventure. ISBN 1-56280-032-9 9.95

A PROPER BURIAL by Pat Welch. 192 pp. Third in the Helen
Black mystery series. ISBN 1-56280-033-7 9.95

SILVERLAKE HEAT: A Novel of Suspense by Carol Schmidt.
240 pp. Rhonda is as hot as Laney's dreams. ISBN 1-56280-031-0 9.95

LOVE, ZENA BETH by Diane Salvatore. 224 pp. The most talked
about lesbian novel of the nineties! ISBN 1-56280-030-2 9.95

THE END OF APRIL by Penny Sumner. 240 pp. A Victoria Cross
Mystery. First in a series.   ISBN 1-56280-007-8   8.95

A FLIGHT OF ANGELS by Sarah Aldridge. 240 pp. Romance set at
the National Gallery of Art   ISBN 1-56280-001-9   9.95

HOUSTON TOWN by Deborah Powell. 208 pp. A Hollis Carpenter
mystery. Second in a series.   ISBN 1-56280-006-X   8.95

KISS AND TELL by Robbi Sommers. 192 pp. Scorching stories by
the author of *Pleasures*.   ISBN 1-56280-005-1   9.95

STILL WATERS by Pat Welch. 208 pp. Second in the Helen
Black mystery series.   ISBN 0-941483-97-5   9.95

MURDER IS GERMANE by Karen Saum. 224 pp. The 2nd
Brigid Donovan mystery.   ISBN 0-941483-98-3   8.95

TO LOVE AGAIN by Evelyn Kennedy. 208 pp. Wildly
romantic love story.   ISBN 0-941483-85-1   9.95

IN THE GAME by Nikki Baker. 192 pp. A Virginia Kelly
mystery. First in a series.   ISBN 01-56280-004-3   9.95

AVALON by Mary Jane Jones. 256 pp. A Lesbian Arthurian
romance.   ISBN 0-941483-96-7   9.95

STRANDED by Camarin Grae. 320 pp. Entertaining, riveting
adventure.   ISBN 0-941483-99-1   9.95

THE DAUGHTERS OF ARTEMIS by Lauren Wright Douglas.
240 pp. Third Caitlin Reece mystery.   ISBN 0-941483-95-9   9.95

CLEARWATER by Catherine Ennis. 176 pp. Romantic secrets
of a small Louisiana town.   ISBN 0-941483-65-7   8.95

THE HALLELUJAH MURDERS by Dorothy Tell. 176 pp.
Second Poppy Dillworth mystery.   ISBN 0-941483-88-6   8.95

ZETA BASE by Judith Alguire. 208 pp. Lesbian triangle
on a future Earth.   ISBN 0-941483-94-0   9.95

SECOND CHANCE by Jackie Calhoun. 256 pp. Contemporary
Lesbian lives and loves.   ISBN 0-941483-93-2   9.95

BENEDICTION by Diane Salvatore. 272 pp. Striking,
contemporary romantic novel.   ISBN 0-941483-90-8   9.95

CALLING RAIN by Karen Marie Christa Minns. 240 pp.
Spellbinding, erotic love story   ISBN 0-941483-87-8   9.95

BLACK IRIS by Jeane Harris. 192 pp. Caroline's hidden past . . .
       ISBN 0-941483-68-1   8.95

TOUCHWOOD by Karin Kallmaker. 240 pp. Loving, May/
December romance.   ISBN 0-941483-76-2   9.95

BAYOU CITY SECRETS by Deborah Powell. 224 pp. A Hollis
Carpenter mystery. First in a series.   ISBN 0-941483-91-6   9.95

COP OUT by Claire McNab. 208 pp. 4th Det. Insp. Carol Ashton
mystery.   ISBN 0-941483-84-3   9.95

LODESTAR by Phyllis Horn. 224 pp. Romantic, fast-moving
adventure.   ISBN 0-941483-83-5   8.95

THE BEVERLY MALIBU by Katherine V. Forrest. 288 pp. A
Kate Delafield Mystery. 3rd in a series.   ISBN 0-941483-48-7   9.95

THAT OLD STUDEBAKER by Lee Lynch. 272 pp. Andy's affair
with Regina and her attachment to her beloved car.
                                            ISBN 0-941483-82-7   9.95

PASSION'S LEGACY by Lori Paige. 224 pp. Sarah is swept into
the arms of Augusta Pym in this delightful historical romance.
                                            ISBN 0-941483-81-9   8.95

THE PROVIDENCE FILE by Amanda Kyle Williams. 256 pp.
Second espionage thriller featuring lesbian agent Madison McGuire
                                            ISBN 0-941483-92-4   8.95

I LEFT MY HEART by Jaye Maiman. 320 pp. A Robin Miller
Mystery. First in a series.   ISBN 0-941483-72-X   9.95

THE PRICE OF SALT by Patricia Highsmith (writing as Claire
Morgan). 288 pp. Classic lesbian novel, first issued in 1952 . . .
acknowledged by its author under her own, very famous, name.
                                            ISBN 1-56280-003-5   9.95

SIDE BY SIDE by Isabel Miller. 256 pp. From beloved author of
Patience and Sarah.   ISBN 0-941483-77-0   9.95

SOUTHBOUND by Sheila Ortiz Taylor. 240 pp. Hilarious sequel
to *Faultline.*   ISBN 0-941483-78-9   8.95

STAYING POWER: LONG TERM LESBIAN COUPLES
by Susan E. Johnson. 352 pp. Joys of coupledom.
                                            ISBN 0-941-483-75-4   12.95

SLICK by Camarin Grae. 304 pp. Exotic, erotic adventure.
                                            ISBN 0-941483-74-6   9.95

NINTH LIFE by Lauren Wright Douglas. 256 pp. A Caitlin
Reece mystery. 2nd in a series.   ISBN 0-941483-50-9   8.95

PLAYERS by Robbi Sommers. 192 pp. Sizzling, erotic novel.
                                            ISBN 0-941483-73-8   9.95

MURDER AT RED ROOK RANCH by Dorothy Tell. 224 pp.
First Poppy Dillworth adventure.   ISBN 0-941483-80-0   8.95

LESBIAN SURVIVAL MANUAL by Rhonda Dicksion.
112 pp. Cartoons!   ISBN 0-941483-71-1   8.95

A ROOM FULL OF WOMEN by Elisabeth Nonas. 256 pp.
Contemporary Lesbian lives.   ISBN 0-941483-69-X   9.95

MURDER IS RELATIVE by Karen Saum. 256 pp. The first
Brigid Donovan mystery.   ISBN 0-941483-70-3   8.95

PRIORITIES by Lynda Lyons 288 pp. Science fiction with
a twist.   ISBN 0-941483-66-5   8.95

THEME FOR DIVERSE INSTRUMENTS by Jane Rule. 208
pp. Powerful romantic lesbian stories.   ISBN 0-941483-63-0   8.95

LESBIAN QUERIES by Hertz & Ertman. 112 pp. The questions
you were too embarrassed to ask.   ISBN 0-941483-67-3   8.95

CLUB 12 by Amanda Kyle Williams. 288 pp. Espionage thriller
featuring a lesbian agent!   ISBN 0-941483-64-9   8.95

DEATH DOWN UNDER by Claire McNab. 240 pp. 3rd Det.
Insp. Carol Ashton mystery.   ISBN 0-941483-39-8   9.95

MONTANA FEATHERS by Penny Hayes. 256 pp. Vivian and
Elizabeth find love in frontier Montana.   ISBN 0-941483-61-4   8.95

CHESAPEAKE PROJECT by Phyllis Horn. 304 pp. Jessie &
Meredith in perilous adventure.   ISBN 0-941483-58-4   8.95

LIFESTYLES by Jackie Calhoun. 224 pp. Contemporary Lesbian
lives and loves.   ISBN 0-941483-57-6   9.95

VIRAGO by Karen Marie Christa Minns. 208 pp. Darsen has
chosen Ginny.   ISBN 0-941483-56-8   8.95

WILDERNESS TREK by Dorothy Tell. 192 pp. Six women on
vacation learning "new" skills.   ISBN 0-941483-60-6   8.95

MURDER BY THE BOOK by Pat Welch. 256 pp. A Helen
Black Mystery. First in a series.   ISBN 0-941483-59-2   9.95

BERRIGAN by Vicki P. McConnell. 176 pp. Youthful Lesbian —
romantic, idealistic Berrigan.   ISBN 0-941483-55-X   8.95

LESBIANS IN GERMANY by Lillian Faderman & B. Eriksson.
128 pp. Fiction, poetry, essays.   ISBN 0-941483-62-2   8.95

THERE'S SOMETHING I'VE BEEN MEANING TO TELL
YOU Ed. by Loralee MacPike. 288 pp. Gay men and lesbians
coming out to their children.   ISBN 0-941483-44-4   9.95

LIFTING BELLY by Gertrude Stein. Ed. by Rebecca Mark. 104
pp. Erotic poetry.   ISBN 0-941483-51-7   8.95

ROSE PENSKI by Roz Perry. 192 pp. Adult lovers in a long-term
relationship.   ISBN 0-941483-37-1   8.95

AFTER THE FIRE by Jane Rule. 256 pp. Warm, human novel
by this incomparable author.   ISBN 0-941483-45-2   8.95

SUE SLATE, PRIVATE EYE by Lee Lynch. 176 pp. The gay
folk of Peacock Alley are all cats.   ISBN 0-941483-52-5   8.95

CHRIS by Randy Salem. 224 pp. Golden oldie. Handsome Chris
and her adventures.   ISBN 0-941483-42-8   8.95

THREE WOMEN by March Hastings. 232 pp. Golden oldie. A
triangle among wealthy sophisticates.   ISBN 0-941483-43-6   8.95

RICE AND BEANS by Valeria Taylor. 232 pp. Love and
romance on poverty row.   ISBN 0-941483-41-X   8.95

OCTOBER OBSESSION by Meredith More. Josie's rich, secret
Lesbian life.   ISBN 0-941483-18-5   8.95

LESBIAN CROSSROADS by Ruth Baetz. 276 pp. Contemporary
Lesbian lives.   ISBN 0-941483-21-5   9.95

BEFORE STONEWALL: THE MAKING OF A GAY AND
LESBIAN COMMUNITY by Andrea Weiss & Greta Schiller.
96 pp., 25 illus.   ISBN 0-941483-20-7   7.95

WE WALK THE BACK OF THE TIGER by Patricia A. Murphy.
192 pp. Romantic Lesbian novel/beginning women's movement.
                                       ISBN 0-941483-13-4   8.95

SUNDAY'S CHILD by Joyce Bright. 216 pp. Lesbian athletics, at
last the novel about sports.   ISBN 0-941483-12-6   8.95

OSTEN'S BAY by Zenobia N. Vole. 204 pp. Sizzling adventure
romance set on Bonaire.   ISBN 0-941483-15-0   8.95

LESSONS IN MURDER by Claire McNab. 216 pp. 1st Det. Inspec.
Carol Ashton mystery — erotic tension!. ISBN 0-941483-14-2   9.95

YELLOWTHROAT by Penny Hayes. 240 pp. Margarita, bandit,
kidnaps Julia.   ISBN 0-941483-10-X   8.95

SAPPHISTRY: THE BOOK OF LESBIAN SEXUALITY by
Pat Califia. 3d edition, revised. 208 pp. ISBN 0-941483-24-X   10.95

CHERISHED LOVE by Evelyn Kennedy. 192 pp. Erotic
Lesbian love story.   ISBN 0-941483-08-8   9.95

LAST SEPTEMBER by Helen R. Hull. 208 pp. Six stories & a
glorious novella.   ISBN 0-941483-09-6   8.95

THE SECRET IN THE BIRD by Camarin Grae. 312 pp. Striking,
psychological suspense novel.   ISBN 0-941483-05-3   8.95

TO THE LIGHTNING by Catherine Ennis. 208 pp. Romantic
Lesbian 'Robinson Crusoe' adventure.   ISBN 0-941483-06-1   8.95

THE OTHER SIDE OF VENUS by Shirley Verel. 224 pp.
Luminous, romantic love story.   ISBN 0-941483-07-X   8.95

DREAMS AND SWORDS by Katherine V. Forrest. 192 pp.
Romantic, erotic, imaginative stories.   ISBN 0-941483-03-7   8.95

MEMORY BOARD by Jane Rule. 336 pp. Memorable novel
about an aging Lesbian couple.   ISBN 0-941483-02-9   9.95

THE ALWAYS ANONYMOUS BEAST by Lauren Wright
Douglas. 224 pp. A Caitlin Reece mystery. First in a series.
                                       ISBN 0-941483-04-5   8.95

SEARCHING FOR SPRING by Patricia A. Murphy. 224 pp.
Novel about the recovery of love.   ISBN 0-941483-00-2   8.95

DUSTY'S QUEEN OF HEARTS DINER by Lee Lynch. 240 pp.
Romantic blue-collar novel.   ISBN 0-941483-01-0   8.95

PARENTS MATTER by Ann Muller. 240 pp. Parents'
relationships with Lesbian daughters and gay sons.
ISBN 0-930044-91-6   9.95

THE PEARLS by Shelley Smith. 176 pp. Passion and fun in
the Caribbean sun.   ISBN 0-930044-93-2   7.95

MAGDALENA by Sarah Aldridge. 352 pp. Epic Lesbian novel
set on three continents.   ISBN 0-930044-99-1   8.95

THE BLACK AND WHITE OF IT by Ann Allen Shockley.
144 pp. Short stories.   ISBN 0-930044-96-7   7.95

SAY JESUS AND COME TO ME by Ann Allen Shockley. 288
pp. Contemporary romance.   ISBN 0-930044-98-3   8.95

LOVING HER by Ann Allen Shockley. 192 pp. Romantic love
story.   ISBN 0-930044-97-5   7.95

MURDER AT THE NIGHTWOOD BAR by Katherine V.
Forrest. 240 pp. A Kate Delafield mystery. Second in a series.
ISBN 0-930044-92-4   9.95

ZOE'S BOOK by Gail Pass. 224 pp. Passionate, obsessive love
story.   ISBN 0-930044-95-9   7.95

WINGED DANCER by Camarin Grae. 228 pp. Erotic Lesbian
adventure story.   ISBN 0-930044-88-6   8.95

PAZ by Camarin Grae. 336 pp. Romantic Lesbian adventurer
with the power to change the world. ISBN 0-930044-89-4   8.95

SOUL SNATCHER by Camarin Grae. 224 pp. A puzzle, an
adventure, a mystery — Lesbian romance.   ISBN 0-930044-90-8   8.95

THE LOVE OF GOOD WOMEN by Isabel Miller. 224 pp.
Long-awaited new novel by the author of the beloved *Patience
and Sarah*.   ISBN 0-930044-81-9   8.95

THE HOUSE AT PELHAM FALLS by Brenda Weathers. 240
pp. Suspenseful Lesbian ghost story.   ISBN 0-930044-79-7   7.95

HOME IN YOUR HANDS by Lee Lynch. 240 pp. More stories
from the author of *Old Dyke Tales*.   ISBN 0-930044-80-0   7.95

EACH HAND A MAP by Anita Skeen. 112 pp. Real-life poems
that touch us all.   ISBN 0-930044-82-7   6.95

SURPLUS by Sylvia Stevenson. 342 pp. A classic early Lesbian
novel.   ISBN 0-930044-78-9   7.95

PEMBROKE PARK by Michelle Martin. 256 pp. Derring-do
and daring romance in Regency England.   ISBN 0-930044-77-0   7.95

THE LONG TRAIL by Penny Hayes. 248 pp. Vivid adventures
of two women in love in the old west.   ISBN 0-930044-76-2   8.95

AN EMERGENCE OF GREEN by Katherine V. Forrest. 288
pp. Powerful novel of sexual discovery.   ISBN 0-930044-69-X   9.95

THE LESBIAN PERIODICALS INDEX edited by Claire
Potter. 432 pp. Author & subject index.   ISBN 0-930044-74-6   29.95

DESERT OF THE HEART by Jane Rule. 224 pp. A classic;
basis for the movie *Desert Hearts*.   ISBN 0-930044-73-8   9.95

SPRING FORWARD/FALL BACK by Sheila Ortiz Taylor.
288 pp. Literary novel of timeless love.   ISBN 0-930044-70-3   7.95

FOR KEEPS by Elisabeth Nonas. 144 pp. Contemporary novel
about losing and finding love.   ISBN 0-930044-71-1   7.95

TORCHLIGHT TO VALHALLA by Gale Wilhelm. 128 pp.
Classic novel by a great Lesbian writer.   ISBN 0-930044-68-1   7.95

LESBIAN NUNS: BREAKING SILENCE edited by Rosemary
Curb and Nancy Manahan. 432 pp. Unprecedented autobiographies
of religious life.   ISBN 0-930044-62-2   9.95

THE SWASHBUCKLER by Lee Lynch. 288 pp. Colorful novel
set in Greenwich Village in the sixties.   ISBN 0-930044-66-5   8.95

MISFORTUNE'S FRIEND by Sarah Aldridge. 320 pp. Histori-
cal Lesbian novel set on two continents.   ISBN 0-930044-67-3   7.95

SEX VARIANT WOMEN IN LITERATURE by Jeannette
Howard Foster. 448 pp. Literary history.   ISBN 0-930044-65-7   8.95

A HOT-EYED MODERATE by Jane Rule. 252 pp. Hard-hitting
essays on gay life; writing; art.   ISBN 0-930044-57-6   7.95

INLAND PASSAGE AND OTHER STORIES by Jane Rule.
288 pp. Wide-ranging new collection.   ISBN 0-930044-56-8   7.95

WE TOO ARE DRIFTING by Gale Wilhelm. 128 pp. Timeless
Lesbian novel, a masterpiece.   ISBN 0-930044-61-4   6.95

AMATEUR CITY by Katherine V. Forrest. 224 pp. A Kate
Delafield mystery. First in a series.   ISBN 0-930044-55-X   9.95

THE SOPHIE HOROWITZ STORY by Sarah Schulman. 176
pp. Engaging novel of madcap intrigue.   ISBN 0-930044-54-1   7.95

THE YOUNG IN ONE ANOTHER'S ARMS by Jane Rule. 224 pp. Classic
Jane Rule.   ISBN 0-930044-53-3   9.95

OLD DYKE TALES by Lee Lynch. 224 pp. Extraordinary
stories of our diverse Lesbian lives.   ISBN 0-930044-51-7   8.95

DAUGHTERS OF A CORAL DAWN by Katherine V. Forrest.
240 pp. Novel set in a Lesbian new world.   ISBN 0-930044-50-9   9.95

AGAINST THE SEASON by Jane Rule. 224 pp. Luminous,
complex novel of interrelationships.   ISBN 0-930044-48-7   8.95

LOVERS IN THE PRESENT AFTERNOON by Kathleen
Fleming. 288 pp. A novel about recovery and growth.
     ISBN 0-930044-46-0   8.95

TOOTHPICK HOUSE by Lee Lynch. 264 pp. Love between
two Lesbians of different classes.   ISBN 0-930044-45-2   7.95

MADAME AURORA by Sarah Aldridge. 256 pp. Historical
novel featuring a charismatic "seer." ISBN 0-930044-44-4   7.95

BLACK LESBIAN IN WHITE AMERICA by Anita Cornwell.
141 pp. Stories, essays, autobiography. ISBN 0-930044-41-X   7.95

CONTRACT WITH THE WORLD by Jane Rule. 340 pp.
Powerful, panoramic novel of gay life. ISBN 0-930044-28-2   9.95

THE NESTING PLACE by Sarah Aldridge. 224 pp. A
three-woman triangle — love conquers all! ISBN 0-930044-26-6   7.95

THIS IS NOT FOR YOU by Jane Rule. 284 pp. A letter to a
beloved is also an intricate novel. ISBN 0-930044-25-8   8.95

FAULTLINE by Sheila Ortiz Taylor. 140 pp. Warm, funny,
literate story of a startling family. ISBN 0-930044-24-X   6.95

ANNA'S COUNTRY by Elizabeth Lang. 208 pp. A woman
finds her Lesbian identity. ISBN 0-930044-19-3   8.95

PRISM by Valerie Taylor. 158 pp. A love affair between two
women in their sixties. ISBN 0-930044-18-5   6.95

OUTLANDER by Jane Rule. 207 pp. Short stories and essays
by one of our finest writers. ISBN 0-930044-17-7   8.95

ALL TRUE LOVERS by Sarah Aldridge. 292 pp. Romantic
novel set in the 1930s and 1940s. ISBN 0-930044-10-X   8.95

CYTHEREA'S BREATH by Sarah Aldridge. 240 pp. Romantic
novel about women's entrance into medicine.
ISBN 0-930044-02-9   6.95

TOTTIE by Sarah Aldridge. 181 pp. Lesbian romance in the
turmoil of the sixties. ISBN 0-930044-01-0   6.95

THE LATECOMER by Sarah Aldridge. 107 pp. A delicate love
story. ISBN 0-930044-00-2   6.95

ODD GIRL OUT by Ann Bannon. ISBN 0-930044-83-5   5.95
I AM A WOMAN 84-3; WOMEN IN THE SHADOWS 85-1;   each
JOURNEY TO A WOMAN 86-X; BEEBO BRINKER 87-8. Golden
oldies about life in Greenwich Village.

JOURNEY TO FULFILLMENT, A WORLD WITHOUT MEN, and   3.95
RETURN TO LESBOS. All by Valerie Taylor   each

These are just a few of the many Naiad Press titles — we are the oldest and
largest lesbian/feminist publishing company in the world. Please request a
complete catalog. We offer personal service; we encourage and welcome direct
mail orders from individuals who have limited access to bookstores carrying
our publications.